American Jihad Rising

Michael A. Elliott

authorHOUSE®

AuthorHouse™
1663 Liberty Drive
Bloomington, IN 47403
www.authorhouse.com
Phone: 1-800-839-8640

First published by AuthorHouse 6/1/2011

ISBN: 978-1-4567-6457-9 (e)
ISBN: 978-1-4567-6458-6 (hc)
ISBN: 978-1-4567-6459-3 (sc)

Library of Congress Control Number: 2011908276

Printed in the United States of America

Any people depicted in stock imagery provided by Thinkstock are models, and such images are being used for illustrative purposes only. Certain stock imagery © Thinkstock.

This book is printed on acid-free paper.

"No matter how well the government says you're protected, the fact is that you and your family are on their own and will be on your own when we are next hit with a large-scale terrorist attack. Plain common sense tells all of us that our nation is too open, has too many targets of opportunity and has a security system too suicidally weakened by political correctness to fully protect us from fanatical terrorists willing to kill themselves in the hope of slaughtering hundreds or thousands of innocent human beings"

-Douglas MacKinnon, "When terrorism hits, don't look to government for help" <u>The Baltimore Sun</u> op-ed page, December 31, 2009

One

Josh finally was prepared to kill another human being.

For the past four months under the expert tutelage of his stepfather he had learned to handle a variety of firearms. Whether it was a .38 revolver, a Glock 19, shotgun or a semi-automatic AR-15 Josh had developed the skill to handle each with deadly accuracy. It had been quite a personal journey because the first time a firearm was discharged in his vicinity, he nearly bawled in fright. As his proficiency increased he grew aware of the yawning disconnect between shooting a static, inanimate object and what would be required of him to target flesh and blood. But the circumstances in which he and his family now lived made his willingness to use these newly-acquired skills mandatory.

Josh and his stepfather, Wayne Foltz, walked along the side of the road after searching for food and other supplies. So much of what passed between them now was unspoken; as if living a stripped down life demanded less verbal communication. It was through a series of near imperceptible gestures that Wayne signaled Josh to come with him. It was dangerous to be out in the open because undiluted evil was on a rampage. Wayne's invitation was all the evidence his 17-year-old stepson needed that he had earned his stepfather's confidence that he could be counted on in an emergency.

As they walked by the burned out and abandoned stores of the Capetowne Shopping Center, Josh gave a glance at what once had been the neighborhood Safeway. It was here that he had been totally mesmerized at the sight of lawyers, teachers, accountants and doctors fighting like feral dogs over basic necessities as panic over world events first took hold. By contrast, Wayne had been a model of cool reserve. Of course, the big-as-a-baseball-bat pistol he brandished assured that whatever he wanted; he obtained without argument or resistance.

Considering how society was collapsing, Josh was puzzled that no one else carried a firearm. He asked Wayne who just shrugged, "They've spent their lives believing the wrong people."

That memory caused Josh to touch the Glock secured in his waistband. He also carried a .38 caliber revolver tucked in a back pocket. Their so-called search for food had largely been unsuccessful because it obviously was not the real reason for this outing. When he asked Wayne why they were so visible his answer was, "We're hunting."

They were bait. They exposed themselves as prey to lure a mostly unseen and unknown enemy to them. They heard the throaty throb of the engine just before they saw the approaching shiny white sedan with the spinners and no visible license plates.

The sedan seemed to slow down, as if its occupants were studying them and assessing the situation. The car would have looked out of place even in normal times. But now its appearance radiated trouble.

Wayne dropped the plastic bags he carried. They didn't break their pace, they didn't stop and they fixed their attention firmly on the white sedan as they walked towards it.

By the way his hands moved under his long coat, Josh knew that Wayne was preparing his pistol grip Mossberg pump action shotgun which was confirmed when he heard the distinctive "click" of a shell being loaded into the chamber.

"Get ready," Wayne said in a near whisper. "Move fast and don't panic. Hold the weapon steady and take your time firing."

Wayne quickly crossed to the other side of the road. The car accelerated towards them. Josh moved into the nearby roadside drainage culvert, dropped to his knees and reached into his waistband.

He wondered if the occupants had a prepared plan of attack. Would they use their car for a series of drive-by attacks or stop and confront them face to face? He flattened himself on the upward slope of the culvert and took careful aim. He'd later recall how steady his hands were. From the sedan came bursts of automatic weapons fire. The shotgun erupted which Josh used as his signal to open fire. He heard and felt ammo slam into the ground around him. Using the roadside ditch as a firing position made Josh a difficult target for even a skilled shooter and these days, Wayne assured him, they were truly rare.

The air vibrated from the firefight. The sedan slowed as it closed in.

The passenger door swung open and a weapons-brandishing Hispanic male emerged; nearly on top of him. Josh quickly discharged multiple rounds from his 30-round clip and the shooter was flung back into the car. The shiny white sedan languidly drifted several feet and rolled into the drainage culvert and the air went silent. Josh started to approach the now stationary vehicle but the weight of Wayne's hand on his shoulder made him stop. Wayne loaded more shells into the shotgun and with it at the ready approached the car.

As he got closer, he pumped three more rounds into the car. After a measured and cautious final approach, Wayne gave an "all clear" signal. By the tattoos that adorned their bodies, tattoos he had seen before, Josh witnessed two very dead Hispanic gang members in the front seat. But it was the body in the back seat that drew his attention. He was Middle Eastern. Wayne very calmly checked the bodies for money, cell phones and other forms of identification. From the jacket of the Middle Eastern corpse, Wayne removed a notebook and, to his surprise, an old-fashioned compass. He quickly flipped through the notebook pages then jammed it and the compass into a coat pocket. He dragged the bodies from the car and piled them into the trunk.

They got into the gangbangers' car and drove off. They would strip it of anything that might be useful and siphon most of the gas. They would take it to Sandy Point State Park and guide the car down one of the many, now unused boat ramps. It would slowly descend and then disappear into the murky waters of the Chesapeake Bay. From there it was a short walk home. During their return, they would take a circuitous route to conceal themselves from view.

"What's the deal with the Arab-looking dude?"

"It's like I suspected. New players are part of the game."

"Seems like they've figured it out and they're closing in."

Wayne nodded. "Yea…I don't think it's a coincidence. By the way, the one gang-banger took several kill shots to the chest. Good work."

Josh smiled. It was better than winning at Madden's NFL Football.

TWO

It was a bright, sunny and warm day in early April so Josh considered it a pleasant surprise when the principal announced that school would be dismissed immediately but that students were not to leave the grounds until a parent picked them up. There would be no buses and even those with private cars would not be allowed to leave.

That last directive brought hoots of derision from the teenage students but when they emerged from the building to find the roadways blocked by the police, they realized something serious was in the works.

When he and others tried using their cell phones, they either didn't work, got busy signals or voice messages saying the system was temporarily out of order. But before he could ponder either development in any depth, Wayne's Ford Excursion SUV pulled up.

Josh got in and was bombarded with a lot of hard to absorb information. There had been a nuclear attack in the Middle East. Israel attacked Iran… or was it the other way around? Either in retaliation or as part of a pre-conceived plan, there were explosions and attacks in cities across the United States including Washington, DC which was only 40 miles from their community located just outside of Annapolis, Maryland. There was a rumor of biological and chemical attacks with thousands dying. Uprisings and attacks had broken out in London and Brussels. Paris was burning. Additionally the North Korean Army had crossed the 36th Parallel into South Korea. Military and communication satellites were mysteriously compromised. Communication centers had been hacked and cyber attacked. Electricity grids across the country had been rendered useless.

Josh couldn't figure it out but it was obvious he was going to have to pay closer attention.

Instead of going home, Wayne drove to a nearby storage company. When he opened the galvanized steel roll-up doors of several adjoining units, Josh was startled by what he saw. Each unit was as large as a two-car garage. There were floor to ceiling stacks of bottled water and canned goods, sacks of flour, rice and powdered milk, seed packets for every type of vegetable imaginable, packs and packs of batteries and what seemed like endless rolls of toilet paper. There were racks of filled propane tanks and a portable generator. But what caught and riveted Josh's attention were the rifles, shotguns and various other types of weapons stacked in a corner. He approached them cautiously.

"They're not loaded," Wayne advised him.

"You didn't get bullets?"

Wayne's opened several foot lockers. Inside each were boxes and boxes of shells, bullets, pistols and revolvers. The overall import of everything contained in the storage units made Josh acutely aware that the rush of recent world events would soon overtake, overwhelm and perhaps destroy those not as prepared as his family would be. Because Josh knew Wayne Foltz was not a frivolous man. He was calm, precise, not given to exaggeration and hyperbole. Somehow he had managed to divine that this level of preparation and stockpiling would be the minimum requirements needed to ride out the approaching storm. Wayne reached into one foot locker for a Glock and handed it to Josh.

"This one I got for you. It's easy to handle with not too much kick, it has a decent range, it's extremely accurate plus it's got deadly stopping power."

Josh refused to take it. The thought of actually using a firearm to injure or kill another living thing made him tremble. He could blow apart alien zombies in a video game with the best of them. What Wayne suggested was too big a leap.

"I don't think I'd be much good with a gun," he quietly protested.

Wayne tossed it back into the foot locker and closed it. "I can understand how you feel but trust me....very soon defending yourself and your mother and your sisters will not be an option."

"But...but...won't you be there to take care of things?"

"Josh, I can't do it alone because I'm the one they'll concentrate on killing first." Wayne paused to see if what he had said made any impression.

It was obvious by Josh's expressions and body language that it was too much, too grim, too unbelievable to absorb in these frantic first moments.

"Let's load the truck and get the hell out of here. We'll get the rest later."

Three

Josh was 7 years old when Wayne Foltz entered his life and now he couldn't remember his first impressions of his future stepfather. As time went on he became acutely aware of the differences between Wayne and his biological father. For one thing, Wayne was older by 13 years. When he and his mom began dating, she was 39-the same age as his dad-and Wayne was 52. And while his father, Phil Andrews, was the epitome of an extrovert, Wayne was quiet and reserved; more of a listener and observer than a talker. Phil, a college English professor, had political and social views that, in the main, were diametrically opposed to Wayne's world view.

The fact Wayne was a decorated Vietnam War veteran and his father spoke against war in any form and for any reason only widen their philosophical gap. Phil had backed his words with action by participating in demonstrations against former president George Bush and the Iraq/Afghanistan wars. During family events like Christmas and birthdays, Phil never missed the opportunity to excoriate Wayne for his military service, his combat experience and his overall support of the American military.

Wayne's typical reaction was to use his superior physical size to loom over his smaller tormentor and stare him down the way one would a child in the middle of a temper tantrum. Josh loved his father but always was embarrassed by his attempts to portray Wayne as a mindless goon.

In the beginning Josh often wondered why his mom, Joanna, was attracted to Wayne. They seemed like a gigantic mismatch. Joanna was a respected therapist and mental health professional while Wayne had his own carpentry business; specializing in hand-made furniture and cabinetry. It surprised Josh to learn that Wayne had a college degree in fine art and his original ambition was to be an artist, a painter specifically. He had paid his own way through college, with the financial cornerstone being a ROTC scholarship. After graduation he had been commissioned a 2nd Lieutenant in the Army and spent nearly two years in Vietnam as a platoon leader. Josh had studied in school that the United States lost the war in Vietnam. In his view, if the other soldiers were similar to his stepfather, he couldn't imagine them losing a war to anyone.

Once, while broaching the subject of his past, Josh asked him what happened to his goal of being a painter. It ended up being an exercise in futility, he was told, because the established art community had no wish to exhibit the work of a baby killer.

Four

On the ride home, Josh asked Wayne to take a detour to his dad's house. Wayne initially wanted to say "no." Phil's house was out of the way and traffic was becoming an increasing problem as the state police and National Guard began setting up traffic checkpoints and detours. Yet, he understood Josh's anxiety.

Phil was sitting on his front porch, as if he were expecting them. He greeted his son warmly but for Wayne he had nothing but his usual political bile.

"Looks like the Zionists have gotten us into a real cluster fuck."

"Nice to see you, too, Phil."

"Seems like you guys finally have the excuse you need to wipe out the international boogey men you've had in your sights for years."

"Well, talking to them obviously hasn't worked," Wayne stopped. There was no point to keep going on this tact. No time for shoulda, coulda, woulda. There were serious issues in the here-and-now that needed to be addressed.

"Look," Wayne continued, "things are going to get dicey real soon. Maybe you should move in with us temporarily; strength in numbers and all that."

Josh was elated by Wayne's offer. "Yea...Dad...c'mon....it'll make Melanie and Katie happy to have you around more. I'd like it too."

"What about your mother? She couldn't wait to throw me out. What makes you think she'd let me back in the door?"

This dredging up of old wounds deflated Josh immediately. "Because it's the best move for you," Wayne insisted. "Your kids want you to be safe."

"From who or what? You don't seriously think we'll be invaded, do you?"

"Who knows? Besides, that's not our biggest immediate worry. It won't be long before the criminals and predators take full advantage of the situation. There's not enough cops and National Guard to protect everyone. I know we're kind of out of the way around here but they'll find us eventually. And you don't want to be out here alone and unarmed."

"I'll be fine."

"Dad!" One short word but Josh's tone was long on despair.

"I'll be fine Josh. Wayne exaggerates."

"But what if he isn't? And if he is, you can always come back."

"I have some extra weapons in the truck. Take a pistol and some ammo."

"Yea, Dad...please!"

Phil went to the Excursion, opened one door and peered inside. He seemed amused in a drool and condescending manner.

"Impressive...in a crazed survivalist sort of way."

Josh, totally crestfallen, walked back to the Excursion and got in. His father's animus toward Wayne fueled by his lingering resentment over the divorce blinded him to the need to be cautious. On their way over, Josh had scanned the AM and FM bands on the truck radio. Those few stations still broadcasting painted increasingly bleak scenarios of what was happening. It really did seem like the world was coming to an end. Wayne contemplated forcing Phil to come with them but the need for unity of purpose would be paramount as events unfolded in the coming weeks. Phil, because of pride and pique, would undermine that needed cohesion. In one last gesture, Wayne loaded a full round of ammo into a .45 caliber revolver and held it out to Phil.

"Take it. It'll help if you get into a jam."

Phil remained unmoved. "How long have you been stockpiling all that stuff?"

"I started the day Obama was elected president. Double downed when he stole his re-election."

Wayne laid the handgun at Phil's feet, got into the Excursion and drove away. Many months later, when it was safer to travel alone, Josh hitched a ride to his father's house. He found it abandoned and ransacked. He would never hear from his father again and he would never learn what happened to him.

Five

Wayne drove home slowly, allowing Josh to cry out all his anguish. He knew what it was like to have events pummel you emotionally to the point where you lose control. The first time he lost men in combat, he spent many hours awash in tears as he wrote the letters informing next-of-kin of the soldier's death. And no matter how many times he did it, it never stopped a rush of crushing pain and regret. As they pulled into the driveway, Joanna and her two daughters, Melanie, 20 and Katie, 18, waved frantically when they spotted the Excursion.

Josh and Wayne looked at each other apprehensively. Jesus, Wayne thought, don't tell me the shit's already hit the fan. Before he came to a full stop, Melanie rushed to the driver's side and in a high-pitched frantic voice tried to explain she had received a one-word text message from Wayne's daughter-in-law, Alison. The word was "help"

Six

With everyone pitching in, they quickly unloaded the Excursion. Wayne handed Josh the Glock and several loaded clips. Josh wanted to protest but under the circumstances, he thought better of it. After Alison's text message was received, the three women tried frantically to reach her by land line and cell phone. Every effort failed and then as they neared the finish, another text message popped up on Melanie's cell. This was from Wayne's daughter, Cindy. She was with Alison and Wayne's grand daughter, trapped in Alison's Baltimore City apartment. Everyone's unspoken question was: Trapped by whom?

Wayne quickly loaded a sawed off shotgun, a Sig Sauer semi-automatic rifle, and a .44 Smith & Wesson Magnum. And from one foot locker he pulled out Kevlar bullet-proof body armor. He kissed everyone and gunned the Excursion towards was Josh feared to imagine.

Seven

The crisis dropped even more surprises on Josh. When Wayne left, he feared that he was expected to be responsible for protecting the family. He held the Glock in one hand and the ammo clips in another when his mother approached and took both from him.

"Here, let me do it for you," she said.

And with practiced ease, she inserted a clip into the Glock, cocked it to load a bullet into the chamber and handed it back to Josh.

"While we're waiting for Wayne to get back, I can show you how to use it."

Josh went totally slack jawed. How could a woman whose professional life emphasized non-aggression and conflict resolution suddenly morph into Lara Croft?

"It's what happened in New Orleans after Katrina," she explained. It was the televised images of people in crisis and chaos, helpless and abandoned by those sworn to protect them and thus left to the tender mercies of the predator class that convinced her Wayne's stance on self defense was not a delusional fantasy of the perpetually paranoid.

So, reluctantly at first, she accompanied him to the shooting range, finally agreeing to professional instruction. She discovered her sense of empowerment was enhanced by her skill with a handgun. If disaster struck, in any form, she and her family would not be cowering potential victims.

"Do Melanie and Katie….?"

"No…but….I'll go over the basics with them….and with Alison and Cindy when they get here."

"And all that stuff in the storage lockers? You knew?"

Joanna smiled and rubbed the top of Josh's head. "Of course, that's not the sort of information married people keep from each other."

Josh had no idea what the future would bring but he did know this was one family it wouldn't pay to fuck with.

Eight

The Excursion didn't drive as much as limp to a stop. A collective wave of anxiety swept over everyone at the sight of a vehicle that looked like it has been dropped from a cliff. It wasn't the dents and gashes not even the near total absence of glass that caused such alarm. It was the bullet holes.

Wayne looked grim, pale and spent as he got out and moved to the rear doors. He reached down into the back foot well and pulled out Emily, his 3-year-old grand daughter. She looked her usual bright and buoyant self; as if she just came from an enjoyable stint at the playground. Next to emerge from the vehicle were Alison, 30, and Cindy, 25. Their faces told a much different story. Alison took a few tentative steps then collapsed crying into Joanna's arms. Melanie rushed to help steady her. Cindy wobbled towards her father; he extended his free arm and pulled her close to him. Josh wondered if he was the only one who spotted the speckled blood spattered across Wayne's face.

"Are you OK?"

"Don't worry, it's not my blood."

Nine

Wayne took it upon himself to form a neighborhood watch committee. Josh was surprised how many people resisted the idea of participating in their self defense. Years of comfort and apathy had dulled their animal senses. There were however, two eager takers. One was Doug McKenna. He fought in Desert Storm and now owned and operated a successful landscaping company. The other was Tom Barton. He served in the 1983 Grenada invasion and was a member of the force that rescued American medical students studying in that island country. He later joined the Anne Arundel County police department and had moved up the ranks to precinct commander. He became one of the department's highest ranked African-Americans until his recent retirement. Through his law enforcement experience and network of contacts he knew how much worse things might become.

In fact, he confirmed Wayne's biggest fear. He had spoken with former colleagues...whenever he could get through to them, the state of communications spotty and erratic at best....and he learned that police forces on every level were charged primarily with protecting government buildings and elected officials and bureaucrats.

The emergency 911 system basically was inoperative. Even if you could get through, responding to the needs of private citizens and providing for their safety and property protection now was a low priority. Weeks later a county police officer stopped by to look in on Tom, who was patrolling the neighborhood with Wayne and Doug with Josh close behind.

Josh noticed the officer made no reference, comment or even alluded to the fact that the three men were openly carrying loaded weapons. Finally, that wasn't surprising because the purpose of the visit was to warn them that nearby communities were experiencing outbreaks of robberies, home invasions and murders. With their forces spread thin over a wide area, there was precious little the police could do to prevent the crime wave, much less do any post-crime investigation. The police officer wished them luck and in his voice was a hint of weary resignation.

Ten

Josh liked Wayne's kids from his first marriage. Besides Cindy, he had a son, Charlie, 29, a Naval Academy graduate now a Navy jet jockey, based on an aircraft carrier in the Persian Gulf. The day before Iran's nuclear attack on Israel, he had communicated with Alison via satellite phone telling her they had been put on combat alert. Wayne guessed his son was airborne striking strategic targets in Iran.

The ability to communicate and receive information steadily degraded day after day. Land lines were totally out, cell phones worked on rare occasions. Television and radio broadcast sporadically and then only news and updates; which did nothing to reduce the collective anxiety. And that was providing electricity was available on any given day. Public utilities were a shambles. They ceased to be upset when they flipped a switch or turned on a tap and nothing happened.

Supermarkets opened sporadically and then for limited hours. Sometimes police were present to maintain order; most times not. Gasoline was in scant supply, the majority of what was available diverted to the military and police. School had been suspended indefinitely out of fear they represented easy terrorist targets. Everyone found Emily to be the type of pleasant distraction needed in such circumstances. Josh noticed how pained Wayne seemed when he looked at her, regretting that the fate of someone so innocent could be influenced by the acts of political maniacs.

One day Josh accompanied Cindy, Alison and Joanna as they took Emily for a walk. Even though they confined their walk to the driveway and courtyard immediately outside their home, Joanna kept a grip on the handgun holstered on her hip. For several days after their rescue, the two young women remained resolutely silent but Josh, gripped by intense curiosity, prevailed upon them to tell what happened.

Cindy who lived in eastern Baltimore County had rushed over to Alison's as soon as she got word of an escalating war. Alison lived in a "nice" section of Baltimore City but like so many urban locations, the nice parts were right next door to the not-so-nice parts. When she arrived, the streets were mostly deserted. Things went downhill quickly. The streets came alive with what she described as "two-legged jackals." The air periodically exploded with the sounds of breaking glass, squealing car alarms and gunfire. Like water seeking its own level, trouble poured out into the streets searching for loot and victims.

Both women frantically worked their cell phones, trying to contact Wayne and his family about their plight. Time after time they failed. They huddled on the living room floor while Emily slept peacefully on a blanket. Alison's apartment building had a secure entrance door but if the electricity failed, there would be nothing to keep out intruders.

Finally, a text message went through. But what if Melanie's cell wasn't on or wasn't working? Hour after hour, the streets seemed to grow more looters and marauders. Cindy's car has been reduced to a hollow metal hulk. Trash barrels were set on fire.

Suddenly Alison's cell burst to life with a text message of salvation, "Wayne coming."

Eleven

Wayne had been stopped at the Baltimore City line by a Maryland State Trooper. There were sealing off the city because of the growing "civil unrest." Wayne's first impulse was to just crash through the wooden barrier. Instead he opted to reason with him, to explain how family members… helpless women, a baby…were in mortal danger.

The trooper was unmoved. Orders were orders. Only police and National Guard were allowed to enter the city. Wayne calmly got out a pad and pencil.

"And you are Trooper….?"

The trooper pointed to his brass nameplate.

"Markey, Trooper First Class Pete Markey."

"What barracks?"

"What are you going to do? Report me to my superiors?"

Wayne met Trooper Markey's smug expression with a rock-hard stare.

"If any harm comes to those women…that baby…I'm going to look you up…give you all the details."

Wayne words had a stun-gun like effect on the trooper. "I'm not a criminal. I'm a father…a grandfather. For the love of God, give me the chance to rescue them."

Trooper Markey glanced into the Excursion. Wayne had made no effort to hide his weapons, leaving them in plain view on the passenger seat. Trooper Markey walked over to the barrier blocking the road, moved it aside and motioned Wayne forward. Wayne stopped long enough to thank the trooper.

"Don't thank me. You're entering hell."

Twelve

Downtown was quiet; the highly-visible saturation of police and National Guard units made sure trouble would be funneled into other areas. It allowed Wayne easy access to the route he needed to reach Alison's. The closer he got, the further he was from the blanket of their protection. More and more people were roaming the streets; loitering, looting and discharging firearms into the air. He placed the shotgun on his lap the semi-automatic and .44 within easy reach. He was moving so he was a target.

The Excursion was pelted with rocks and anything the mob could hurl at it. As more people choked the streets, he was forced to slow down. He was determined not to be stopped. If that happened, the mob would swarm over him. He might not end up dead but the rescue would fail.

He rolled down the driver side window, pointed the shotgun in the direction he was driving and fired over the heads of the crowd. The noise of the shotgun blast and the whistle of buckshot caused the crowd to duck and disperse opening up more of the street.

It also brought a new hail of debris at the Excursion. Then a bullet shattered a rear window. He could hear it ricocheting in the rear storage area. The stakes were being raised as people, enraged by his tactics, began chasing after him. The momentary opening on the street began to disappear. This time he fired directly into the crowd. As bodies toppled and people scattered, he accelerated. He could hear and sense bullets striking the Excursion. He could see more people giving chase.

He accelerated again, using the shotgun to clear the road in front of him. Even at a faster pace, he was having difficulty putting distance between himself and his pursuers. People were racing to reach the driver's window. He grabbed the. 44 and just waving it out of the window caused people to give up the chase. He fired a round over their heads just to emphasize the point.

A large SUV barreling down the street forced people to yield. The roar of the shotgun and the damage it was doing had the desired effect. As he drove faster, Wayne maneuvered the Excursion to avoid a direct strike on a pedestrian. He feared a body would get wedged in the under carriage and bring the Excursion to a disastrous halt. With rocks, bricks, bottles and cans hammering the vehicle, Wayne finally saw the opening he needed and temporarily sped out of harm's way.

Thirteen

Every fleeting second heightened Alison's fear that the formless, restless mob would find their way into the building. Cindy was anxious too but for different reasons. She always admired her father's courage and resourcefulness but if what was happening in the streets below was being replicated throughout the city, she wondered how he could possibly get all the way uptown. She shuddered but not out of concern for herself but from her understanding that Wayne would not hesitate to leave a trail of blood and destruction in his wake.

In the distance, she heard the blare of a horn. This wasn't one of the random soundings they had heard on and off throughout the hours they had hunkered down in the apartment. This was rhythmic and purposeful. The women looked at each other and began gathering up what they needed to make their quick escape

Wayne knew the horn would attract unwanted attention but he didn't have time or the option to run up to the apartment and ring the doorbell. Again, the mere sight of the .44 discouraged those who had thoughts of rushing the SUV. He drove the Excursion up onto the sidewalk and as close as possible to the apartment building's front entrance. He gave the horn one last, long blast then exited firing the Sig Sauer to scatter the pressing crowd. The effect was only momentary. The mob was like waves at the beach, as quick as they retreat they reform. Wayne made the next burst of fire more purposeful. He squeezed off individual shots and put down several menacing looking types as a full demonstration of his willingness to survive by deadly means. Again, the desired effect was only temporary. Soon, the mob would find the collective courage and fury needed to overrun him.

"Dad! Dad!" Cindy and Alison, clutching Emily in her arms, burst through the front entrance.

"Get in the back, down on the floor. Hurry!" Wayne yelled.

He edged away from the slowly approaching mob. Hurled paving stones shattered and crumpled the Excursion's rear tailgate and rocker panels. Wayne fired off a burst in a semi-circular pattern. People toppled, the mob hesitated, scattered. Suddenly return fire came from the direction of the apartment building. They weren't aiming at him. They were concentrating fire on the Excursion's engine and tires. Wayne hopped in, threw the idling vehicle into drive and sped away. The Excursion absorbed damage from virtually every direction. People tried blocking their escape. Cindy could feel the SUV shudder with each collision. Glass shattered and sprinkled them like jagged snowflakes.

She heard her father yelling, "Get off! Get off!" She worked up the courage to peek over the center console between the bucket seats. Some determined man was on the hood, slowly crawling towards the windshield. Wayne jerked the steering wheel left and right trying to dislodge him but with no success. Finally, gripping the windshield wiper arms, he pulled himself forward and began pounding on the windshield. Wayne raised the .44 in plain sight but the intruder made no effort to stop his assault. Wayne hesitated for a few seconds and then fired through the windshield. The intruder vanished; leaving behind only his blood.

Cindy then swallowed a scream as another intruder managed to land on the Excursion's running board, punch her father in the head and attempt to gain control of the steering wheel. The surprise assault caused Wayne to lose his grip on the .44 and it tumbled into the passenger side foot well.

The struggle over the steering wheel and Wayne's attempt to reach for any weapon caused the Excursion to sway dangerously. Cindy reached over the passenger seat to grab the sawed off shotgun that had slid between the passenger seat and the door. She got it close to Wayne's hand. He grabbed it and using it like a club struck the intruder several times in the face with the butt end. But this person possessed a determination beyond reason. He grabbed the shotgun and tried to wrest it from Wayne's grasp. He had it with both hands while Wayne was limited to one. The tug-of-war seemed destined to end in a crash or worse.

Cindy leaned over to help because Wayne was losing the struggle. The shotgun was just 2 feet long so she could only grab that small area between the combatants. She wrapped her hands around the weapon and strained to break the intruder's hold. He punched her squarely on the side of her face. She fell backwards but did not immediately let go. The momentum shift, coupled with the intruder releasing his two-handed grip, allowed Wayne to regain full control of the weapon. Cindy would long remember that what immediately followed seemed like a freeze-frame from an animated 3-D movie; something so surreally vivid that she could forever describe it in the minutest detail.

Wayne fired point blank at the intruder's face. The skin, from the top of his head down to his finger-tips vaporized, revealing his skeleton. It was so finely detailed that it struck her as being an illustration from a medical text book. Then with blood, bone and all manner of fluids splaying the Excursion's interior, he was gone.

Cindy, suppressing the urge to vomit, threw herself down on the rear floor huddling next to Alison who steadfastly maintained her body as Emily's shield. She began to pray in a manner she hadn't experienced since Catholic elementary school and wondered if they had made a strategic blunder; abandoning what seemed like the relative safety of the apartment building for a rolling metal coffin. From behind came the unmistakable electronic whine of a police cruiser. The Excursion stopped and she heard the squealing of brakes and the slamming of car doors. Her initial expectation was the police had been sent to apprehend the madman in the SUV. But there were no shouts, no commands. She dared to peek again from between the bucket seats and saw her father in conversation with several police officers who stood at the open driver's side window. After a few moments, the police returned to their cruisers, fired up the lights and sirens and took off with the Excursion close behind.

"We're getting an escort out of town," Wayne shouted. "Let's hope this thing holds together and gets us home."

The Excursion now rested off to the side at the top of the driveway. It had been transformed from a vehicle to a kinetic metal sculpture reflective of the deadly and uncertain world this family…and millions of other families…now inhabited. Their neighborhood stroll had taken them to this spot and they had walked around it and examined it as Cindy concluded her story.

"I use to give Wayne such grief over this," Alison said. "How dare he drive such an oversized gas-hog that contributed to global warming." She paused, reflecting on how such ideas had once held sway over society. "All I can say now is thank God he didn't show up in a Prius."

Josh had listened to all this with a feverish concentration. Cindy's vivid description of their ordeal left him breathless. The women continued their conversation but he broke away, quickly entered the house and bounded up the stairs to his bedroom. From the closet shelf he retrieved the Glock and the extra ammo clips.

Hoping back down the stairs, he found Wayne reading on the back deck. Josh showed him the weapon. "I want to learn how to use this."

Fourteen

Down a winding road bordered on both sides by thick woods a visitor would arrive at the community of "Chesapeake Heights." Situated at the junction of the Severn River and Chesapeake Bay, its topography and terrain had been shaped 180 million years earlier as receding glaciers and ice floes elevated beds of sandstone and shale to heights as much as 125 feet above the water surface. Centuries of constant, rapid water flow carved and eroded the edges of this land mass and exposed it to seasonal freezing of water in its cracks and crevices. Sections of shale regularly and steadily broke off and tumbled into the water. The collective effect was that over time these smaller pieces weathered into a massive rock wall that steadily rose up the sides to become a sheer and formidable barrier.

Eventually, this fusion of geological collisions and upheavals assumed a semi-circular shape that jutted far into both the bay and river, towering above the water; a green and lush escarpment that stood in near-solitary splendor to its immediate surroundings.

As was the custom in the 17th Century in the original 13 Colonies, this land was deeded to minor English nobility in return for the crops grown and the resulting taxes they generated. Through 4 generations, it remained the possession of the Emory family until 1878 when George Emory sold it and adjoining plots to one Horace Waveland as a means to settle a variety of gambling debts. Emory sold the large parcel for 50 cents an acre and bragged he got the better of the deal.

From the outset, Horace Waveland utilized the land to grow tobacco. After a few bumper crops, tobacco made him one of the wealthiest men in Maryland. History has shown that eventually dynasties are undermined by descendants whose members fail to maintain the passion and vision of the founding generation. Family scion Matthew Waveland spent the greater part of the 1960s finding his "groove", ingesting acid and its various derivatives in Haight-Ashbury and making frequent trips to India to bask in the aura of the Maharishi Mahesh Yogi and, hopefully, to share an ashram with members of the Beatles. Eventually, the land was seized by the IRS for failure to pay taxes and sold to a local real estate developer.

The early Chesapeake Heights residents, enamored of the old growth forest that surrounded and defined the area, created and contributed to a trust fund that eventually was used to buy the near-pristine wooded acreage from the developer; assuring they would never lose the splendid isolation and beauty their woodlands provided.

Upon entering the community, the pastoral theme was maintained over several acres of open land highlighted by gardens and walking paths. One had to travel around a long, winding curve to gain first sight of homes, the pool, clubhouse and tennis courts.

The blended Foltz-Andrews family had moved into a comfortable, 4-bedroom single home three years earlier. Josh thought it was a definite upgrade from the older townhouse they lived in after his parents divorced. In was a friendly place, in the typical modern suburban way. Neighbors knew each other in a superficial, non-committed manner. People said hello, waved and engaged, when they had to, in mindless chit-chat about unimportant topics.

These days Josh found a severe attitude shift regarding his family. The major focus fell on his stepfather. Words like "vigilante", "gun nut" and "criminal" were used routinely. Even his mother was subject to whispered disapproval, even outrage. Despite all that had happened... was happening...even with the stark symbolism provided by the bullet-mauled Excursion, people were alarmed that Joanna was instructing her son, daughters and stepdaughters in the use of firearms. During many afternoons, the neighborhood reverberated with the "pop, pop, pop" of small arms fire as the family backyard had been transformed into a target range.

Josh noticed how much the women enjoyed their increasing proficiency with firearms. It brought them an obvious sense of calm, confidence and surety in an increasingly chaotic world. During one particularly raucous target practice session, Josh was struck with how the women had become so assertive and vocal. That piece of expertly crafted metal they held in their hands liberated them from that pall of fear so palatable in the rest of the community. And Wayne's words to him about how he might someday be the last line in their defense no longer filled him with terror. As he watched the women he was overcome with a deepening sense of love and duty. Even though he was just past his 17th birthday, Josh Andrews had discovered that cause worth dying for.

Fifteen

A neighbor confronted Wayne about the backyard firing range; threatening to call the police. That threat amounted to no more than comedic irony because there were no police. During one of their regular neighborhood patrols, Tom Barton revealed that as the national crisis lengthened with no immediate end in sight, county and state police increasingly were failing to report for duty. They were choosing, instead, to stay at home to guard their families and property. At night, police precincts essentially stood empty.

Whether or not these residents of Chesapeake Heights were willing to face it, maintaining law and order now fell to each individual.

Wayne, Tom and Doug attempted to recruit additional members to the neighborhood patrol. The typical responses were doors shut in their faces, a desire not to "get involved", an aversion to guns, the "my wife won't let me" excuse. The excuse Josh found most amusing and perplexing was the accusation that the three men were lawless vigilantes. Through it all, the men maintained their poise and their determination not to waver from their mission and that included a pledge to defend those who choose not to defend themselves. This wall of denial didn't stand too long before it was breached by reality that showed up in several different forms.

Sixteen

The reaction to a knock on the door now was to reach for a weapon, approach the door quickly and cautiously with the weapon at your side and the safety off. Josh had to suppress laughter when he realized that from the foyer to the dining room, everyone was on alert with a weapon in hand. No more assuming the person at the door is the friendly pizza delivery man.

It was Tom Barton. With him was a couple not from the neighborhood. They were Alan and Laura Charles who had become, in essence, refugees. They had lived in a very upscale development located approximately 25 miles up the nearest main highway. They had fled to stay with friends at Chesapeake Heights because their idyllic little corner of the world had been invaded by the 21st Century version of the barbarian hordes. At first it was break-ins, a mugging in broad daylight and when it became apparent few knew how to cope with this onslaught it escalated into all-out lawlessness. Those who could flee did so, leaving everything behind. But with gas not easily available, many families were stuck in place and became convenient targets.

These were not spontaneous mobs looking for and reacting to crimes of opportunity. They were organized gangs that struck with purpose. Every night…and even during the day…new variations of urbanized terror took place. The ultimate horror occurred when during a home invasion a man was dragged into his front yard and in front of his wife and children was pummeled to near death. There were no police to stop this atrocity …no EMTs to whisk him to a life-saving hospital…and no one brave enough or equipped to fight back. Even behind closed doors, no one escaped the man's pleas for help and then his inevitable death rattle.

With hope gone and help unavailable, the Charles' abandoned their home and struck out on foot for anything that resembled safety. They were not the only ones. Along their circuitous route away from the main roads they encountered neighbors and strangers. An army of the upper-middle-class reduced to zombie-like wandering. Mrs. Charles began sobbing. They're somewhere in their mid-30s, Joanna thought, yet they now seemed older by decades.

"Why didn't you escape by car?" Wayne asked.

"They would siphon the gas out of people's cars or just punch a hole in the gas tank and drain it," Mr. Charles related. "This family...the Bensons...tried it. Apparently they only made it a mile or so before they ran out of gas. The next day, car was there...they weren't. Five people... vanished."

Seventeen

They ate their meager dinner quietly. The women claimed to have found a silver lining to this situation, saying they now were approaching their ideal weight. Alison declared she had finally managed to shed the leftover poundage she attributed to child birth. Only Emily was spared any depravation.

Tom and Doug showed up after dinner. The arrival of the Charles' and several other refugee families was the harbinger they all feared.

"We're dealing with elements of MS-13 and a lot of wannbes Hispanic gangs out of northern Virginia and Montgomery County. That's the main force behind what's happening," Tom said. "The FBI and county and state police gang units have monitored them for years, watched them double in size while they were protected by all these groups worried about their civil rights. This is their breakout moment."

"Northern Virginia? That means they're pretty mobile even with all the shortages," Wayne observed.

"They hijack cars not for the cars but for whatever fuel they can get," Doug explained. "Then they double up and travel in vans and pickups."

"A couple of them will roll into an area to scout things out," Tom continued. "If it looks promising, they sweep in like a plague of locust… and we've heard how that plays out eventually."

Josh found himself choking back a rising panic. Until now it had all seemed so other-worldly; the danger was out "there" in some nebulous universe that had no real connection to his personal reality. Now it was rolling their way and it was savage and merciless. The fact these men could speak of it so detached and casually only increased his anxiety. They were warriors who had personal dealings with combat and death. They would not panic. They would not run. But the grim quietness of their conversation meant they understood clearly how dire things might become.

"Well, we're going to be badly outnumbered no matter what," Wayne said. "Until they show up, we're going to have to wait and react."

"If they're anything like the Zeta drug gangs, they're lethal and highly organized with a military style chain of command," Doug added. "We may have to adopt guerilla tactics to compensate for our lack of numbers and firepower."

"Let me ask you something," Wayne continued. "How much fun was Desert Storm? I envied you guys. Took the offensive…never gave it up. Rolled over those motherfuckers like they were made of cardboard. Buried them alive in their bunkers….shot them all to hell as they retreated back into Iraq."

"Yea, the Highway of Death…it was quite a show."

"In Vietnam, command once ordered us to set up a fire base so close to North Vietnamese positions, you could spit and hit them. The official name was Fire Base Hercules…but we called it Fire Base Little Big Horn."

The men laughed that laugh of recognition and of shared pain and loss.

Eighteen

Josh leaned on his shovel and looked over at Wayne. He couldn't recall if Wayne was 64 or even older but he admired his physical capabilities. Even though it was hot and the air thick with humidity, Wayne worked his shovel tirelessly. They were in the 6th week of the crisis and the disposal of garbage and human waste had emerged as a major health concern. In the beginning many in the community had placed their garbage and recycling on the curb as usual. When it repeatedly was not picked up and eventually ripened on the sidewalks they reacted with anger and demanded an investigation.

Reliable running water and sewage now were items relegated to the status of nostalgic longing. With toilets reduced to dry, useless porcelain decorations Wayne and Tom organized work crews to create locations where the pungent, bacteria loaded and vermin attracting output of increasingly primitive living could be safely deposited.

Josh observed that the same people who responded to the concept of being responsible for their defense also were the ones doing the back-breaking work of creating latrine pits and mini-landfills. He complained to Wayne and said that a system should be devised that would prohibit those who didn't work from using the hand-dug sanitary facilities.

Wayne dismissed the idea immediately. "We have more important things to worry about than who the latest pile of shit belongs to." While excrement sailed under his stepfather's radar, issues of food and water occupied space near the top of the list.

He had stockpiled what he estimated to be a 3-4 month supply. That was based on 5 adults. The addition of two adults and one young child shortened that time frame considerably. In the early stages of the crisis, Wayne organized raiding parties that looted local supermarkets, warehouses, convenience stores and even hijacked delivery trucks. The results were never as bountiful as they had hoped but it added to a stockpile that was distributed to those most in need.

Joanna and the women planted a sizeable backyard garden with an emphasis on starchy foods loaded with carbohydrates. Wayne had built a fence with a gate to keep 4-legged critters from stealing the results of their hard work. As for 2-legged critters, everyone in the family was instructed first to fire a warning shot and if that failed then attempt to wound the intruder. Wayne assured them there would be no criticism or recriminations if their marksmanship was not precise and their shots proved fatal.

Nineteen

The attitude among the majority of the neighbors had changed dramatically. The Charles' story and the experiences of other refugees spread like a deadly virus. Fear with an undertone of panic had violently intruded into everyone's life.

Now, when Wayne patrolled the area, people called out to him… stopped and engaged in conversation designed to elicit his view of future events…thanked him for his vigilance. Josh heard no more name calling, no snide or snarky comments, no more whispers that Wayne was a misguided reactionary leading people astray.

The afternoon target practice sessions in the backyard became a clarion call that more people heeded. Tom and Doug attended every session because Wayne needed their help to manage the growing number of people seeking firearms and instructions. Still, there were those who resisted the notion of being involved in their own self protection. They were polite yet firm in their belief that their non-involvement and good intentions somehow would cause the Angel of Death to pass over their homes.

Wayne laughingly called them "bitter clingers" but neither he nor anyone else ever suggested these people were not worthy of their protection and would be left defenseless.

Josh came to understand why Wayne's all-time favorite movie was "The Magnificent Seven." A morality play set in the old West it told a story of 7 skilled gunmen for hire who agree, for only a $20 gold piece each, to rid a poor Mexican village of the bandit gang that regularly terrorized them and stole precious crops needed to sustain their families.

What motivated them was the quest for redemption. They willingly performed the ultimate act of contrition to atone for lives devoted to dealing out death by quietly accepting the fate of their own certain and unheralded deaths in a distant and desolate farming village. Even when betrayed by frightened villagers and their lives spared by the bandit chief, Calvera, they returned to finish their "contract" to rid the village of the bandit scourge. The present situation brought to Josh's mind the response of the cowardly gunman, Lee, who when told he didn't need to return to the village because "you don't owe anything to anyone," answered, "except to myself."

This is what animated his stepfather and his two brothers-in-arms. As young men they learned everything about death before they barely understood life. And now buried deep in their DNA was the unrealized need to prove that the deaths they caused were right and just and their souls were free from that sin. To prove their worthiness they'd defend not only family, friends and loved ones but people who mocked them, who wouldn't even thank them for the risks they assumed.

Later that night, Josh sat alone in his room and in the dim light of a lantern aimed his unloaded weapon at imaginary foes. He felt fear crawl up from his belly and begin squeezing the breath from his lungs. He always was certain others would fold and run when pulling the trigger meant the difference between life and death. But now he didn't know about himself. Would he stand fast, hold his ground and help the others repel any invaders? He didn't know…he couldn't tell….he couldn't convince himself that he wouldn't run at the first blast of hostile gunfire. His new passion was to comb through the history books in Wayne's library and become acquainted with great and consequential military actions and battles. From Thermopylae to Stalingrad to the Battle of The Bulge, he immersed himself in the strategy and tactics that lead to victory. He became obsessed with the warrior mentality and how it steeled men to put aside their fear of death.

How could men in ancient times meet face to face and hack each other with swords and battle axes? What level of courage did it take for the men at the Alamo to stand fast and fight to a bitter end and the Confederates at Gettysburg to make Pickett's Charge? How could men of the Greatest Generation storm the beaches at Normandy and Iwo Jima? Each and every combatant, known and unknown, throughout history had faced that moment. How in the name of God did they find their courage? Josh asked himself repeatedly. He couldn't begin to imagine. And when fear had squeezed the last breath from his body, he gulped deeply and vomited on himself.

Twenty

For years afterwards, everyone involved in the incident would swear they were the first to hear the cries for help. Yet no one disputed that Wayne was the first one out the door, sprinting towards the sounds of distress; a .45caliber Smith & Wesson at the ready.

Josh followed not too far behind and he was joined by most of the women. Up ahead in the next courtyard he saw three people struggling. As he got closer, he recognized Mr. Matthews grappling with two Hispanic males outside of his Lexus SUV. In the next instant there was a gunshot and Mr. Matthews collapsed to the ground. Wayne accelerated towards the scene. The Hispanic on the driver's side spotted his approach, turned and fired. In response to this fusillade Wayne stopped and fired off two rounds. The Hispanic bounced back against the Lexus and flopped forward.

The second Hispanic male attempted to flee but the gunfire had alerted Doug McKenna and other neighbors who immediately cut off his first route of escape. He attempted to double back but Wayne's quick approach with a raised .45 persuaded him to drop his own weapon and surrender. Even though he had been rendered momentarily harmless, no one approached him. They stood back and merely examined this heavily tattooed young male with a mixture of apprehension and curiosity.

"Jack Matthews is dead," Tom proclaimed. "Shot right in the heart." The announcement caused a tremendous collective gasp; tears were mixed with yelps of outrage and calls for revenge.

And the perp?" Wayne asked.

"Dead before he hit the pavement. These jokers are MS-13. They've got all the tats and markings…prison time, murder….the complete MS-13 honor roll."

The crowd had grown larger by the moment but abruptly all the conversational buzz ended as people stepped aside to allow Patricia Matthews and her 16-year-old daughter, Brittany, to pass. From the looks on their faces, it was apparent someone had rushed to give them the news. Joanna intercepted them, spoke quietly and briefly and then stood by helplessly while the two women dissolved into mournful heaps. Others came forward to help support and comfort them. The entire situation now had been infused with a supercharged level of emotion and anger.

Wayne spotted Rosalie Perez, a Spanish teacher at the high school, in the crowd. Her husband's Army Reserve Unit had been called to active duty two weeks before the attacks which indicated to most people that the government knew hostile action was in the works. It was anyone's guess whether anyone anticipated how extensive and damaging those attacks would be.

"Mrs. Perez," Wayne called out to her, "Would you please ask him what he's doing here and what he's looking for?"

She came forward and spoke to the captive in a gentle tone but despite the fact he was surrounded, his expression spoke of total scorn and disrespect. Even though Josh couldn't understand a word, every syllable conveyed his hatred.

"He says they are the new Conquistadors. That their will to conquer has always been strong but now they have the means to make it a reality and that with their allies they will crush the Anglos and their lackeys and take their rightful place in world affairs."

"Ask him who he means by 'allies'?" Doug asked.

Mrs. Perez asked the question but the prisoner refused to answer.

"What are we going to do with him?" called out someone from the crowd. This set off a chain reaction of questions and statements dealing with a variety of issues from what to do with the dead bodies, to calling authorities, to lamenting the fact that no one in what could be loosely-characterized as authority had been visible in weeks.

"Everyone back away from him," Wayne ordered. When people were slow to respond, he yelled. "I said get away from him! Now!"

The tone in his voice worried Joanna, "Wayne...what are you going to do?"

"Has anyone been able to get through to 9-1-1 lately? Doug?"

"All I get is constant dead air and that's providing I can even get a signal or a dial tone," he answered.

"Anyone else been able to get through to 9-1-1?" Wayne continued.

He already knew the answer but people in the crowd continued to call out suggestions on alternate courses of action. The one idea that reached a quick consensus was to transport him to the nearest county police station and turn him over to authorities…provided, of course, the station was manned adequately and he could be properly confined.

"What do you think, Tom? Is the Millersville precinct operational? Glen Burnie or Pasadena?"

"It's a coin flip but the smart money says 'no'. My worry would be safely transporting this goon and then what to do with him if we can't find a station that's totally up, running and secure."

While elements of the crowd reignited the debate over what to do with the surviving gangbanger, Wayne's attention was focused on the Matthews women who clung to friends and neighbors as they were led away. At one point, Wayne's line of sight caught not only the women but the unremorseful thug whose eyes followed them and sparkled with a malevolent glee that showed how much he enjoyed the misery he had visited upon them.

"Mrs. Perez," Wayne's tone sucked the crowd noise from the air. Josh experienced an involuntary shudder. His stepfather had revealed himself in many different ways during this crisis and now Josh was prepared to discover what he was certain would be another

"Mrs. Perez," he repeated. "I want you to ask him once again what he wants and tell him if he hopes to live, not to go into another geo-political rant."

Mrs. Perez asked and the gangbanger seemed amused by the life-or-death condition Wayne had placed on answering the question. His answer obviously caused Mrs. Perez major discomfort. She looked at Wayne but said nothing. Then she engaged the gangbanger in some additional conversation. While the actual content was hidden in Spanish, Mrs. Perez's body language and the stress in her voice only spread tension and apprehension among those gathered…except for Wayne. Josh was riveted watching his stepfather remain so calm and in control. But he could feel his flesh begin to tingle with that mixture of fear and excitement because he instinctively knew Wayne's outward appearance masked a boiling rage.

"Well?"

Mrs. Perez took a few quick steps in Wayne's direction. At first Josh thought she was going to plead for mercy. Then it struck him she was moving out of the line of fire.

"Why is he here? What does he want?"

"He says he is here for blood."

Josh heard the shot even before it was fired because all his senses instantly anticipated his stepfather's response. The .45 caliber slug struck the gangbanger just to right of his heart. His face registered shock and then…was that a knowing smile that crossed his lips?

Did he realize that Wayne had avoided an instant kill shot so that he would live long enough to anticipate his own death? It seemed that he crumpled to the ground slowly, as if his last act would be an attempt to defy the laws of gravity and remain upright as long as possible.

He lay on the ground; his breathing became more rapid and labored. Josh had never seen another person shot, much less die. He was surprised that his only reaction was satisfaction. He looked in the direction of his family. His mother and the other women seemed to share his emotional detachment. What became manifestly obvious was the demarcation between the dueling "camps" in the neighborhood was now open and clear cut.

On one side stood his family, the Bartons, the McKennas and those individuals and families who had become regulars at the backyard target range, took part in armed neighborhood patrols, attended regular strategy and tactical meetings and attended to the garbage and latrine pits. As today's drama had unfolded, others had drifted…deliberately or unconsciously…to the side fully determined to use every means necessary to defend themselves.

On the other side stood those equally determined to deny the danger that was closing in on them. "You're a murderer!" screamed a female voice. Monica Hastings emerged from the crowd. Joanna wasn't surprised that she would speak out. They had been close friends when the family first moved into the development. It seemed a natural bonding; a mental health professional and a liberal criminal defense attorney. But rifts developed over Joanna's growing attachment to a more conservative world-view.

Monica rushed up to Wayne and continued her tirade. "You killed him in cold blood! You had no right to do that."

Wayne looked at her with that look of frustration that adults use when trying to reason with an emotional teenager who believes they are the source of all knowledge.

"You're right Monica. I should have water boarded him instead."

"I swear to God Wayne. I'm going to make sure you don't get away with this."

"What the hell was he supposed to do?" Doug entered the dispute. "Let him go so he could bring back his homies?"

"We could have placed him under citizen's arrest and held him for the police."

Doug nearly broke out into laughter. "Held him? Where? Your house?" He gestured towards the crowd. "Anyone of you willing to take him in as a house guest?" He redirected towards Monica. "He was a world-class thug, a murderer. You could have tied him up, chained him up…whatever. But sooner or later he'd have gotten free and hung around long enough to slit your throat." Before he could continue, Wayne pulled him away. Doug looked at Wayne who merely shook his head.

"I'm not kidding Wayne. I'm going to see you're brought to justice on this."

Josh watched his mother's face turn explosive red with anger. She and his sisters began to move forward but Wayne waved them off and they stopped. Josh increasingly was captivated by the way so many people now followed his stepfather's every direction.

He huddled with Doug, Tom, his mother and others who had begun to play more prominent roles in what many were calling "Foltz's Army."

"We're done here for now," Tom Barton proclaimed to the crowd. The authority inherent in his voice and body language caused some grumbling and restlessness but as an experienced leader, he was unmoved. "Look, I spent 25 years devoted to maintaining law and order. No one believes in it more than I do. But what's happening now has changed everything. We either respond to the new reality or get destroyed by it."

The weight of those words crushed the final notes of complaint. He formed a committee to conduct a proper burial for Jack Matthews. Wayne and Doug McKenna set out to locate whatever vehicle had brought the menace right to their doorstep. They then would set out to erase all traces of their existence and prepare for the next encounter.

Twenty-One

The pre-teens and teenagers that lived in the community gathered at the community pool at twilight. The fading light shimmered in the algae-chocked water that sat in the pool's bottom. Although it was well into summer, enjoying idyllic, lazy summer days had entered the realm of fantasy. These occasional gatherings were a combination bull and information-sharing session. Josh had become the headline attraction because of his family. At first, he enjoyed the spotlight but as circumstances became more dangerous, he chose to be more circumspect and introverted. Seeing three men die that day had a jolting effect, even though he did his best to hide it. But some of the others treated it as if it were a movie highlight.

"Josh man, your stepdad is like a killing machine. Bang! Bang! Two dead spics,"

"He doesn't enjoy it, Randy. He does it because he has to."

"Still, I wish I could shoot like that."

"Come over one day. He'll give you a weapon and show you how to use it."

The invitation caused Randy to look down at the ground then at some of the other young males. When he spoke, he couldn't look directly at Josh.

"I've wanted to but my dad wouldn't let me."

"What about now, especially after what happened today?"

"I asked but he won't allow guns in the house, said violence never solved anything."

Josh decided this was not the time to start an argument. He decided to emulate his stepfather and try to win the day with the calm force of a persuasive argument.

"What about you?" Josh spoke to a boy named Adam Pecora.

"My mom feels the same way. Said it's best to give a burglar what they want. Having a gun might just make them mad."

"Besides," Randy continued, "my dad said what your stepdad did today only made matters worse. Those gangs will be out for revenge."

"And that makes the case for being armed even stronger."

Randy shrugged. "Maybe...but dad said when the time comes, they'll realize we had nothing to do with killing those dudes and they'd go gunning for you and the McKennas and the rest."

"If those creeps roll into this neighborhood, what do you think is gonna happen? They're not gonna go door to door and take a survey. Words and good intentions don't stop people like that"

"So what are we suppose to do?" asked Adam.

"Get a gun, learn to use it."

"I can't disobey my parents like that," Randy protested.

"You have to...you have to protect yourself. You have to protect your family. Those guys today...and their buddies...they're like Orcs. All they care about is killing. You've heard the stories. When they kick in the front door and go for your mom and your sister..." When Josh saw the looks on his friends' faces, he stopped. Their faces showed a fear anchored in the no-longer-deniable reality of their circumstances.

"My dad..."

"What do you mean...your dad? " Adam cut him off, almost annoyed at Josh's mistake. "He's your stepdad!"

Right...right..." Josh quickly corrected himself. "He'll give you what you need...show you how to use it. Keep it with you. Don't tell your folks... when the time comes, you'll know what to do."

The others nodded. He motioned that they should follow him to his house. They walked without speaking which gave Josh the opportunity to think about his slip of the tongue. He wondered if his brain was rewiring itself. The closeness and cohesion of his family unit had made distinctions based on blood irrelevant. The task of assuring their self-preservation had redrawn the lines of kinship so that any artificially imposed societal distinction between each individual had been totally obliterated. Debating whether Wayne should be identified as his father or stepfather now seemed trivial and irrelevant. Because when danger and death arrived, he'd be there; ready to take a bullet to save anyone of them. That, Josh decided, was all he needed to know to accord Wayne Foltz his filial loyalty.

Twenty-Two

Families began leaving in significant numbers. The fear generated by the day's events motivated those who, essentially, were unprepared to cope with what would almost certainly be more attacks. In the first days of the crisis, other families packed their vehicles and fled but most seemed willing to stay put and ride out what they thought would be a series of minor inconveniences. Now it was abundantly clear there would be no figurative cavalry riding to the rescue.

Wayne, Tom and Doug waited at the community entrance attempting to dissuade them from leaving. The crisis, now in its 12th week, supported their conclusion no safety could be found on the road. During the preceding weeks, the three men spent time on Wayne's shortwave radio in regular contact with amateur radio operators across the country. The reports they received created a forlorn picture of a nation gripped by anarchy and combat. Many urban areas were smoldering ruins from the effects of small nuclear and dirty bombs. Houston, Phoenix and major portions of the southwest were under siege by what was said to be elements of the Mexican Army. Among the enemy dead, it was claimed, were combatants from Cuba and Venezuela.

All semblances of structured order and authority had disappeared. They had been replaced by tribal-like factions formed along the lines of neighborhoods and families to provide self-defense and survival. Their neighbors who wanted to leave had no plan, no weapons, and no idea of a final destination. They just felt compelled to "get away." With no way to distinguish friend from foe, their chances were less than minimal.

They successfully persuaded many not to allow their panic to become a death sentence. It was far safer, they argued, to stay and prepare themselves collectively for whatever may come. Many others, however, decided to push on. What in the world will happen to these people, Tom wondered silently. Even though he asked the question, he really didn't want the answer.

Twenty-Three

It wasn't easy transforming a home into a fortress. Even though he possessed building skills, Wayne found the lack of essential materials difficult but not impossible to overcome. He spent a moment examining the finishing touches that converted Joanna's walk-in closet into a safe room. He had replaced the flimsy interior door with two solid exterior doors. Between the two doors he installed a long, thick granite slab. He had scavenged these items from abandoned homes. It was the same throughout the community. Most abandoned homes were stripped down to their frames as everyone looked for whatever material they could use to keep bullets and invaders from gaining access. He also had cut apart their washer and dryer plus several others and used the sheet metal to reinforce the interior walls. The hardest part had been cutting through an exterior wall to create an airway passage.

This was the final piece of construction. Lower floor windows, auxiliary doors, patio sliders and the garage door had been rendered, to the best of his ability, inaccessible. Only two front windows, the front door and the kitchen door leading to the upper deck were left free to open and close. And even these could be barricaded shut with only minimal effort. The major downside was that as the summer heat built, every fortified house assumed the still air of a crypt making life just that much more unpleasant.

He was surprised by the sudden appearance of Melanie and Katie. Even though they were 2 years apart he always thought of them as twins. They were blessed with their mother's good looks and temperament. They were defined more by their common interests than any differences. And they were the least approving of his courting and eventual marriage to their mother.

While Josh adopted a wait-and-see attitude, the young women were immediately vocal and negative. Much of it was attributable to the natural emotional fallout from the divorce. They were devoted to their father and even though Joanna had been single for nearly 2 years, Wayne's arrival signaled that the girls' fanciful, hoped-for reconciliation between mother and father would never materialize.

They zeroed in on the 13-year age difference to suggest this was an ill-conceived relationship. Wayne actually admired the cleverness and high level of abstract thinking they used to bolster their arguments. Wayne once asked a then 12-year-old Katie why she found the age gap so bothersome. She looked at him with all the confidence and self-assurance she possessed and said, "How would like it if I started dating a 25-year-old man? Wouldn't you try and stop it?" Wayne found the core of her argument difficult to challenge. Other salient age-related facts tossed at him included, "When you graduated from college, mom was in elementary school", "The first time you got married, mom was in middle school" and "when Charlie was born, she just started high school."

Wayne accepted it all with a large, much needed measure of good humor. The turning point in his relationship with the 2 girls occurred when he accompanied Katie during soccer signup. They had just moved to Chesapeake Heights and everyone at the local recreation center involved in the sign-up process assumed him to be Katie's father and addressed him as such, much to Katie's silent dismay.

A few days before the first game Katie confided to Joanna she would rather not have Wayne come and be forced to listen to people call him her dad. Wayne's response was to have a t-shirt embroidered with "Not Katie Andrews' Dad". When he emerged from the bedroom on game day wearing that t-shirt he was greeted by all the kids with glee and laughter and became a welcomed fixture on the sidelines.

"Is there room in here for all of us?" Melanie asked as the girls peered into the closet turned safe room.

"It'll hold most of us plus enough food and water for three to four days."

"Most of us?

"I estimate it can hold 7 ½ people with no problem."

"You'd stay outside?"

They stared at him blankly. He knew this was no time to sugarcoat the truth or to minimize the stakes.

"If I felt it was necessary. Look, it's a simple equation. Let's suppose five guys break in. If all of us squeeze into the closet, it leaves 5 guys running loose to cause havoc. But if I'm outside, I can pick off at least two of them. The rest would probably run away. At worst, you'd only have to deal with three…not five."

Katie gave him a hug. She took Melanie's hand and they started to leave.

"If we survive, it'll be because of you…everything you've done… everything you've taught us. We're glad it's you. We're glad it's you that's here with us."

Twenty-Four

The knock on the door he had expected for weeks finally arrived. For Fareed Akbari it meant that this was his moment to make a critical contribution to the defense of his friends and neighbors. Chesapeake Heights was home to several families with origins and ties to the Middle East but Dr. Akbari, a renowned vascular surgeon at Johns Hopkins Hospital, was the informal leader of this group.

He was born in Iran in 1961 to a prosperous merchant family. Members of the extended Akbari family were cultural but not religious Muslims. The men were educated in London, Paris and Brussels. The women were more at home at Harrods or on the Champs-Elyse than on Tehran's Valiasr Avenue. They were immersed in commerce, travel and consumption; totally comfortable with the Western influences that permeated Iran during the reign of the Shah. Fareed remembered fasting during Muslim religious holidays but only a few times in his life did he ever enter a mosque.

A student at Columbia University when the Shah was deposed; he watched with dismay and heartbreak as Iran fell into the grip of Muslim fundamentalism and the iron rule of the mullahs. He especially reviled those who stormed the American embassy and held hostages for 444 days.

The revolution shattered his close-knit family. They managed to leave Iran with the majority of their assets and settled in Egypt, Turkey, France and England. He ignored his parents' repeated entreaties to join them in Paris. Fareed loved America so he became an American. Now, more than 30 years from the moment he raised his right hand and swore allegiance to the U.S. Constitution and to defend it and his adopted country from its enemies, he knew they were all in peril from the same forces that propelled Iran from a beachhead of Western rationalism into a rabid theocracy.

In the beginning of the crisis when he was needed to perform critical surgery, he had been driven to Hopkins by the police or elements of the National Guard. Located in the heart of an east Baltimore ghetto, it had been spared from attack during past urban riots; the locals apparently appreciating its international status. This time it was different. The hospital was subjected to hit-and-run attacks by armed and highly-organized marauders. They were a flash mob with automatic weapons and rocket launchers; suddenly appearing, sowing fear and havoc then seemingly melting into the air. More disturbing than the attacks was the nature of the attackers. Physicians and nurses who tended to those that were wounded and captured noted with great unease they were either Hispanic or of some Arab lineage. Dr. Akbari understood what everyone feared to say; the hospital was a terrorist target.

The contingent of police and Guardsmen assigned to protect them seemed up to the task of coping with this hit-and-run strategy. Until the suicide bombings began. First they targeted the hospital staff, then the police. Soon, fewer police showed up for duty, shifting the burden to the already understaffed National Guard unit.

No matter how far they pushed back and extended the perimeter, no matter how many barricades were erected, the suicide bombings continued. Even when such attacks "failed" they succeeded in frightening and demoralizing the entire hospital population. Then an extended lull in the attacks began to stir hopes that the worst was over; until an explosive-laden ambulance was driven right up to the emergency entrance. No one ever bothered to count the number of people killed and wounded, nor was a dollar amount ever attached to the damage caused by the subsequent fires and mini-explosions. The military commanders decided that defending Johns Hopkins now was unsustainable. The most prestigious hospital in the world was abandoned. Patients were transferred to other hospitals deemed more defensible. The medical and support staffs were left to their individually-determined fates.

From the outset he was one of Wayne's most passionate and vocal supporters. His entire family...wife Fatima and sons Amir, 19 and Hassen, 22...were among the first to receive firearms training. His sons took an active role in the armed neighborhood patrols and they all attended the regular neighborhood defense meetings. When the monsters devoured his native country, he could only watch helplessly. Now, they were coming for his beloved adopted homeland and he was prepared to shed his blood to the death in its defense.

Twenty-Five

In a world where the soft ubiquitous hum of electricity and the ceaseless roar of the internal combustion engine had been silenced, any and every loud random sound was cause for concern. Several people spotted Wayne and Josh leaving the community that morning. Word spread quickly and all were left to speculate why. Even Joanna was left without an explanation. The sounds of their firefight, even though miles away, rippled through Chesapeake Heights in all its brief and explosive fury. The stagnant summer heat kept people outside so there was no lack of an audience. Yet when silence returned no one spoke or commented because nameless fear obligated them to wait until the outcome was certain.

When they returned hours later, there was a mixture of relief and apprehension. While everyone was grateful Wayne and Josh were unharmed it now was obvious that the second bloodletting in less than 48 hours would undoubtedly be followed by more. As they passed among well-wishers, Wayne spotted Fareed and motioned to him. "We need to talk with you about something really important," was all Wayne said.

Fareed opened the door and Wayne, Tom and Doug entered. Fareed noticed that Wayne moved slowly and appeared slightly stooped, as if he were bending under the weight of his command responsibilities. He handed Fareed the dead Arab's journal.

"We need to know what this says."

Twenty-Six

The journal was written in Fareed's native tongue. He read silently and the more he read, the more his soul drifted into despair.

"This is a detailed journal and there's not a shred of good news in it," was Fareed's initial comment.

"Just give us the highlights," Wayne responded.

Fareed released a low sigh, almost a moan. "This is the journal of Naser Mikailli, an officer in the IRG; the Iranian Revolutionary Guard. He arrived in America a little more than 2 years ago. He traveled from Tehran to Venezuela and after six months in Caracas, he journeyed through Central America into Mexico where he linked up with his 'Mexican brothers united in the struggle against Western imperialism.'"

"Guess that's who the gangbanger meant when he mentioned 'allies,'" Tom interjected.

"Members of the Zetas smuggled Naser across the border into Arizona and he's been in this country ever since."

"Doing?"

"Contacting and uniting existing sleeper cells in anticipation of what he calls The Day of the Great Reckoning."

"Nice of them to give it a formal title," Doug said.

"Here's the really disturbing part," Fareed continued. "He writes they're forming a rather sizeable force…an army if you will…uniting Hispanic gangs, elements of Hamas, the Muslim Brotherhood and the IRG with the goal of conquering and subjugating the local population."

"That's fucking crazy," Doug snapped. "Do they really think they can defeat and conquer us from within?"

"He writes that Allah will guide them in this quest and lead them to an ultimate victory."

"True believers…they're nearly impossible to defeat. I faced them in Victnam. They'd sacrifice and suffer anything for their cause. No matter how many we killed, they still kept coming. Our notions of life and death meant nothing to them. In Vietnam, I was part of a special tactical unit formed to intercept North Vietnamese Army arms shipments. One night we set up an ambush on the Trang Li River. Well, someone must have tipped off the NVA because…."

They waited for Wayne to continue. Instead, he appeared to retreat into some deep interior recess of forgetfulness.

"And then what happened?" Doug asked.

"It's not important. It's just that we can be damn sure these Islamic fanatics are worse."

"We're really in the deep shit," Tom said quietly.

Fareed handed the journal back to Wayne.

"Anything else in here important?"

"The rest is mainly his descriptions of how they plan on dealing with the conquered infidels. It's best left unspoken."

"If Hamas and the IRG are plotting tactics and strategy then we're talking about a force that's organized and cohesive," was Doug's analysis.

"And they'll be better equipped. Now we have to worry about not only being outnumbered but also being out-gunned," Tom added. "How do we counter these advantages?"

Wayne leafed through the notebook as his comrades spoke.

"Maybe we need to hit them first…launch a surprise attack."

The other men looked at each other as if they had just listened to the proclamation of a mad man. Wayne caught their looks and he approached Fareed, pointing to a double spread section of the notebook.

"These lines and arrows…do they have any particular meaning?"

"None that I could see, that's why I didn't mention them."

Wayne stared hard at those pages. The others saw his eyes beam with a sudden look of recognition. He reached into his pants pocket and pulled out the compass.

"It's a hand-drawn map…a map in progress. With no GPS or cell phones working consistently…they're as blind as we are. So, while they're searching for their two missing comrades, the Arab was charting the streets they were on for future reference."

Wayne placed the journal on the coffee table. Fareed, Tom and Doug gathered close to it and examined the previously cryptic drawings.

"That's why the Arab carried a compass. See...," Wayne oriented the compass with the hand-drawn arrows. "That's east and west, so that makes this long continuous line College Parkway and these crossing lines...Green Haven Road...Belle Rive Drive...Bay Dale...and the last one...Cape Road where Josh and I encountered them."

"If they don't know where we are...then we don't know where they are," was Doug's immediate conclusion.

"Sure we do," Wayne quickly countered. "Just follow the College Parkway line to where it bends and then, according to the arrows, swings north up Ritchie Highway...."

"Where it stops at the intersection of Robinson Road," Doug continued.

"Let's assume that's the starting point."

"That leaves an awfully big area where they might be."

"But it does put them where the Charles' and the other refugees said they are located," Tom added. "But no one we debriefed ever mentioned seeing anyone that looked like they were from the Middle East."

"They've been sitting tight, waiting for the arrival of Hamas and IRG fighters and a new command structure. It's like the Arab wrote in the journal, they're still putting together their army" Wayne concluded.

"And you really think we should hit them first?" Doug asked, almost rhetorically.

"We don't have a choice. They sent two people out on a reconnaissance mission. When they didn't return, they sent out these last three. We have maybe 12 hours before our friends realize those three aren't coming back either. They'll come out in force next time. If we hit them guerilla style, we have a chance to inflict some damage. Take a bite out of their asses."

The other men nodded. Guided by their military experience, they instinctively knew it was the correct move.

"I want to go with you," Fareed declared

"Absolutely not," Wayne said firmly. "You're much too valuable to risk losing you in this type of operation. There's going to be war casualties very soon and your skills will save lives."

"Then take my sons."

"No, they're brave and eager but they're not ready. Don't be impatient. The opportunity for vengeance will be here soon enough."

Fareed nodded and accepted Wayne's judgment. He then embraced his friends individually.

"God be with you. The sword of Allah is on the march and none of us will be spared."

Wayne motioned to Tom and Doug that they should leave. Once outside he told them. "We leave at sunset."

Twenty-Seven

During the few intervening hours, they recruited several other men in the community to join in the mission. They limited it to those who had evolved into "regulars" at target practice and self defense meetings. They finally settled on three; Jim Barnes who had served four years in the Coast Guard. The only "combat" he had ever experienced was a shoot out with drug smugglers off Key West. Still, he was weapons trained by the military. Bill Griffith had almost completed police academy training when the war suspended life as he knew it and the academy was closed indefinitely. He was only 22 but Tom was confident he'd act and react in the ways required.

The third addition was Alan Charles. Ever since he arrived he had been an enthusiastic participant in weapons training, becoming well-versed with a variety of firearms. He would be the patrol point man. He would lead them back to his old neighborhood, re-tracing the route he and others had used to escape undetected.

Wayne had concerns about his participation. He was a man decidedly out for revenge; an emotional luxury they couldn't afford under the circumstances. But he was determined to join them and they needed his ability to guide them to the right place.

They had conducted the search in as low key a fashion as possible and asked each man to swear his family members to secrecy about what was planned. Wayne feared that if Monica Hastings and her allies found out, they'd do anything possible to thwart them, perhaps even warning the IRG-lead thugs an attack was coming; all in a misguided attempt to stop the violence. Wayne decided being paranoid was needed this time.

When they were assembled at his house for a briefing, he surprised everyone by handing out night-vision goggles and Kevlar body armor. But he saved the biggest surprise for last. Wayne unveiled the jewels of his weapons collection...six fully-automatic AK 47s. The sight of these combat icons drew low whistles and mumbles of excitement and appreciation.

He had become a fan of the AK 47 when he relieved a dead North Vietnamese Army soldier of his. Throughout the U.S. military in Vietnam, the AK was admired for its ease of use, accuracy and near indestructibility. He carried it with him into the field despite orders from commanding officers to abandon his "commie weapon." But he was steadfast in his defiance, a stance that earned him the respect of the men in his platoon. They too were inspired to acquire AKs from North Vietnamese soldiers who obviously had no further use for them.

They were kept hidden until now because he worried they would generate fear and panic among the uninitiated. They might have derailed his plans to create a neighborhood defense force; so potent was the animosity towards this weapon.

Only days before the country was attacked, when the airwaves and talking head shows were crackling with news of the North Korean Army massing on its border with South Korea; of the Israeli Defense Force on high alert and closing its borders; with President Obama assuring the American people that the leaders of these hostile nations had given him personal assurances they only sought peace with their neighbors, Wayne and Joanna were dining at one of Annapolis' finest seafood restaurants.

At the table next to theirs was a group of 20-somethings who were discussing current events and politics in an extremely lively and loud fashion. At one point the discussion turned to the 2nd Amendment. Out of 6 people, only one defended the absolute right of the individual to bear arms. One scholarly wag proclaimed loudly and in self-righteous indignation, "why would anyone want an AK-47?"

Wayne was tempted to provide the answer but decided the young man would discover it himself soon enough.

Twenty-Eight

Wayne watched the bright tropical sun retreat quickly behind the jungle canopy. Virtually at his feet the Trang Li River flowed lazily towards the south. He studied the map enough times to know his 8-man fire team was well within Cambodia. For two nights and a day, they had waited patiently for the first moonless night. Intelligence reports indicated the North Vietnamese Army had turned the Trang Li into an arms highway during the moon's dark cycle.

It was such bullshit, he thought. Every officer and grunt in country knew that this war was drawing to a slow close. Nixon had promised as much during his re-election campaign. Once the political bigwigs solved such critical issues like the size and shape of the negotiating table, the Paris Peace Talks guaranteed that South Vietnam would be sacrificed in an elaborate diplomatic kabuki dance designed to obscure and deny the truth.

Interdicting this shipment of NVA arms would have no real impact on the overall weapons build-up designed to smash the South Vietnamese Army and conquer the country. It all was political theater that would get glowingly written up in some report that would be fed to an increasingly disinterested American public claiming how American military efforts were making a critical difference. Of course, the part about the action actually occurring in Cambodia would be conveniently omitted.

Still, Wayne had no trouble volunteering his squad for this type of mission. Compared to humping in the bush, this was a relatively safe assignment. They had been inserted by Swift Boat a few clicks upriver 36 hours earlier and quickly made their way to this narrow river bend to set up their ambush. They waited in total silence; communicating only by

61

tugs on the rope that bound each man to the other. They did not swat the bugs and mosquitoes that constantly assaulted them. The previous night the river's high tide had engulfed them waist deep. Yet they absorbed all the punishment nature meted out because it meant their ultimate survival. They could not risk a single act that might betray their presence. When the small boats made their way past, their actions would be swift, lethal and final. Then they quickly would retreat back upriver to be extracted by Swift Boat before the main NVA force could assemble to intercept them.

Wayne's weapon of choice for such an attack was a double-barreled sawed off shotgun. In close quarters it was hideously effective. No living thing could survive its massive kill force. He rubbed his hands over it constantly while waiting. Every nick, scratch, ding and dent provided a tactile reminder of enemies confronted and destroyed. Wayne drifted off to catch a quick nap. The NVA would be on the move tonight. He would be ready.

Wayne was awakened by the tug of the rope. He tugged back in response, cut himself free and moved to give himself a clear line of fire. Even in the thick, moonless dark he could distinguish the outline of the river and hear the sounds of paddles softly breaking the water's surface. As commanding officer it was his responsibly to initiate fire. He counted four boats and waited patiently for the lead boat to be directly opposite the shotgun's barrels. As he squeezed the trigger, his boot slipped slightly in the soft mud. This caused him to miss the center of his target and the boat was merely grazed at one end. But the report of his shotgun set off the appropriate firestorm. The quiet jungle night suddenly roared like a frightful beast. Only the brief screams of the dying provided any counterpoint.

Wayne watched in disbelief as the lead boat continued to move downstream. He leapt into the river while reloading. The river was deeper and the current stronger than he anticipated. But he could not let the boat escape. Then the current cooperated by sending the boat into the near bank. He quickly drew closer. As he raised the shotgun, he was confronted by the outline of a human figure suddenly standing in the boat. He stifled a laugh, "Could you make it any fucking easier?" he thought. The shotgun erupted. The body disappeared.

He approached the boat from the riverbank. There was no movement and he unloaded two more rounds into it as a precaution then briefly illuminated the scene with his Zippo. The body in the boat was a woman. He probed it with the shotgun and was startled to hear a small, soft cry.

Beneath the woman's ripped and lifeless body was a small child alive but seriously wounded. There were no weapons in this boat or any of them. They had slaughtered a contingent of women, old men and children; decoys sent down river by the NVA to be sacrificed in order to foil the American ambush.

Now exposed, they had no choice but to race to the pickup point and avoid capture; leaving the river free for the actual arms shipment. The horror of this event sank so deeply into each soldier they instinctively agreed to report the ambush a total success.

Sitting on his deck, preparing for battle, watching a blazing tropical-like sun set over the Severn River forced Wayne to retrieve that night from deep in his memory. While he had suppressed it at Fareed's, the realization they would be engaging a vile foe who had no regard for human life forced it out. And with it the understanding that victory and survival required they meet this enemy with an accelerated measure of viciousness that would block out completely their ingrained predisposition to be merciful.

Twenty-Nine

They were an hour into their trek walking cautiously and deliberately through the total darkness. At their current planned pace, Wayne estimated they'd arrive at their destination around 2am; Charlie-time as it was known in Vietnam. Even though it was 40 plus years since he last slogged through the jungle, this had some of that familiar feeling. It was oppressively hot and humid. Weighed down by body armor, various weapons of choice in addition to the AK 47, ammo and rucksacks, the late August weather provided another layer of discomfort. They maintained complete silence through the woods to conceal their presence. When they found themselves in the open, they quickened their pace to return to cover ground as quickly as possible. When they needed to cross a road, they did it one man at a time and in rapid succession. And they were heading to engage an enemy whose location and combat strength were largely mysteries.

While in country, Wayne grew to grudgingly admire the Viet Cong and North Vietnamese soldiers. They were tough and determined bastards. In 1995, the 20th anniversary of the fall of Saigon, he had been part of a contingent of Viet veterans to visit on a goodwill mission. He and his comrades spent much time with their counterparts, revisiting battle sites and reliving the events that helped reshape the destinies of two disparate nations. No matter whom he talked to from the other side; from lowly ammo runner to field command officers, one theme emerged transcendent above all others. The Americans had the numbers, the weapons and the technology to win the war but they were betrayed by their political elite who bowed to public pressure.

It was Wayne's hope that the exploration would permit him to finally banish the ghosts of those soldiers that died under his command. That they died in vain meant the loss he felt would ebb over time but would never totally leave him. As he listened to his footfalls he linked the past to the present. Now as then he was engaged in combat because of a lack of political will in dealing with savage and criminal nation states. His thoughts drifted to the early 60s anti-war folk song, "Where Have All the Flowers Gone?" He found a bitter irony in the song's refrain, "When will they ever learn? When will they ever learn?" A very good question... when indeed?

Thirty

He never could have imagined himself as a 60-plus warrior. What he found surprising was how good he felt. The need to ration food has caused him to lose 35 pounds over the course of 4 months. No one was spared that reality. Everyone had lost considerable weight. At least the war would cure America's obesity problem. But he also lost those nagging aches and pains so common when one passes 50 and 60. He couldn't figure out if it was because those maladies were psychological or because of the radical changes in diet. Whatever the cause, he knew others who experienced the same relief. Tom had retired several years earlier than he had anticipated because of a bad back that now he professed was totally healed.

The change in his physical well-being now made him deeply regret that he had passed on acquiring a 30 caliber Browning Automatic Rifle. The BAR was a vaunted light machine gun that could wipe out a squad in one burst. But he had feared he didn't have the strength or endurance to handle it properly. But now he felt physically reborn, something he couldn't have anticipated. Too bad, he mused, a BAR undoubtedly would now prove useful.

Thirty-One

Josh turned on the mini-flashlight so often Joanna warned him he risked wearing out its precious battery power. He repeatedly checked the time on his wrist watch, trying to form a mental picture of how close his stepfather's patrol was to their target. This mattered because Josh was part of the extraction team. While the patrol followed a circuitous route on foot to avoid detection and create a surprise attack, their retreat needed to be swift and motorized.

Two high-powered vehicles were fully fueled and, like the stagecoaches of the old west, there would be a driver and a gunman riding shotgun. Josh was so disappointed he wasn't included in the assault force he begged for the chance to be part of the extraction team. Wayne hesitated at first but relented, despite his wife's quiet protest. Josh had handled himself well during the last shootout and Wayne felt he deserved to take his place with the men.

Again, he nervously checked his watch. It said "1:15". Precise time had become another casualty of the war. It was left to each group of people to frame time in whatever context was meaningful. Everyone had synchronized their watches so no matter the actual time, they were all on the same clock.

Besides his Glock, Josh would also carry an AR-15. He gathered together his weapons and ammo, kissed all the women good-bye and set off to meet Joe Wiggins, the driver. He was a 30-something auto mechanic who had joined the self-defense movement early on. They would be using the late Jack Matthews' Lexus SUV. When they had gone to the Matthews home to get it, Brittany Matthews pulled Josh aside to wish him well. She finished by kissing him on the lips and said, "For my sake, I want you to kill as many of those bastards as you can." It wasn't Romeo & Juliet but it made Josh's heart flutter.

Thirty-Two

They emerged from the woods that bordered on what had been the luxury community's private golf course. They paused to listen but heard only nature's night sounds. They advanced slowly towards the cluster of houses that Alan Charles said the gangs had requisitioned for their own use. They stopped at the tee for the 13th hole and dropped to a kneeling position. They were well out of range but they had a clear and unobstructed view of the houses. Wayne removed binoculars from his rucksack.

"I don't see any sentries," Wayne said. "How about dogs?"

"Never saw any."

"Big dogs cost a lot to feed, probably couldn't afford it," Tom added.

Wayne was staring down a dead end residential street that slopped downward a few degrees and ended at a manmade earth wall built to shield the end houses from road noise. It had been planted and landscaped but months of neglect and dry conditions reduced the growth to piles of tinder. This would be their escape route. There were 8 homes to his right, 6 to the left. In front of four different houses and up the driveways were enough vehicles to indicate they were occupied.

"What's your best guess which house is being used as command headquarters?"

"Our right, 4th house from the corner."

"How sure are you?"

"It's my house or was my house. They came in, made us virtual prisoners…had to feed them… wait on them, watch how they terrorized the neighborhood. We were lucky to escape with our lives."

"How many do you think we'll find?

"15-20…there's 4 bedrooms and a big family room downstairs."

"Any other home we should hit?"

"The house to the left of mine and the one directly across the street."

Wayne had everyone resynchronize their watches. First, they would work in teams to disable as many vehicles as possible to eliminate immediate pursuit. Then they would attack the homes commando style and kill as many of the enemy as possible before they could muster their forces. Wayne had worried about inadvertently killing innocent civilians that still might live in these homes as captives. Alan assured him that anyone held against their will for this long would welcome death. Wayne gave the thumbs up sign. Everyone nodded and they moved out.

Thirty-Three

Two teams of three worked each side of the street quickly and cautiously. Every tire was slashed. If hoods could be opened wires were ripped out and stuffed in a rucksack so they couldn't be reused. If a hood couldn't be opened, sand and dirt was funneled down the fuel pipe. It was decided not to risk going after those vehicles parked up in driveways. They would be dealt with when the firefight started. When they were done, they retreated back to the golf course to finalize their assault.

According to Alan's information, three houses presented themselves as prime targets but their numbers precluded striking all three at once. It was decided to hit Alan's old home and the one to its left. Wayne and Bill Griffith would attack the main target, Doug and Jim Barnes the other. Tom and Alan would provide cover from the street. They moved out silently crossing the once finely manicured front lawns, approaching the front of each house slowly and deliberately. They paused to allow Tom and Alan to assume a defensive support position. After they were in place, each team approached their target.

Wayne tried the doorknob. He wasn't surprised to find it unlocked. It pushed open silently and he stepped inside. He listened for any sounds of activity. Through the goggles he saw nothing that indicated human presence. He motioned Bill Griffith to follow him. Standing in the foyer, they were confronted with a multitude of choices. A wide staircase to the second floor and all the bedrooms was to their right. They were standing at the beginning of a hallway that lead to what Wayne assumed was the kitchen and family room. He decided to move down the hallway to the rear of the house.

He peered into the kitchen or what once resembled one. It was trashed and littered to an extent that Wayne feared going in any further for fear of kicking a bottle or can that might rouse anyone nearby. He spotted an open door that according to Alan's description lead to a finished basement. It would be necessary to determine if anyone were downstairs. If so, they'd have to be dispatched to avoid being surrounded when they attacked upstairs. He signaled he was moving forward and guided by his aided vision, he tip-toed gingerly amidst the debris to the door.

Wayne stared down the darkened stairs. Never in his life did he wish more for some glimmer of light. That absence among all the other deprivations suffered over the past months was the one he missed most. Nights were dreadful and even for the bravest, full of unknown perils. He dreaded the shortening days that signaled the arrival of fall and colder weather.

The stairs were carpeted so he was confident he could tread softly enough to avoid being discovered. When Wayne got to the bottom of the steps, he paused and drew a deep silent breath. He pivoted to his left, the AK-47 ready to deliver the final judgment in quick, short bursts. Instead, what he found caused him to freeze in amazement.

The entire space was filled with portable, infantry-style weapons of every possible description. There were Uzis and Mac-10s, 60mm machine guns, BARs plus crates of one-man surface-to-surface, anti-tank missiles, grenade and rocket launchers. Wayne stood at the edge of a massive armory designed for overwhelming firepower from highly mobile forces.

For the first time since this conflict placed ordinary citizens in jeopardy within their own neighborhoods, Wayne felt a deep, numbing fear. Given that there may be 30-50 enemy combatants in this immediate area, the number and diversity of weapons confirmed the menace Fareed found in the journal of Naser Mikailli. This was not the signature of a rag-tag gang of thugs but of a force set upon annihilation. The gangbanger he had killed spoke of being out for blood. Wayne now feared it would be measured in more misery than anyone could imagine.

Thirty-Four

Tom and Alan had settled down in front of a chest high stone fence that sat at the bottom of a steep, sloped front yard. The house was set back so far if anyone came charging out of it, they most likely would be out of range. It was an ideal spot. They had an unobstructed view of the two houses and it provided protection from rear fire. Tom squinted through his goggles to catch a glimpse of Wayne and Bill entering their target. He worried about the potential success of this mission. He found it more than ironic that he was more in more danger on this suburban lawn then he ever was in Grenada.

In the tomb-like silence he prayed for their survival. What no one would ever know was that in his prayers he bargained with God; offering his life in exchange for Wayne's. Many in the neighborhood were baffled and upset because Tom never assumed the lead in building the self-defense team and tactics. After all he was a combat veteran, a decorated police officer and precinct commander; a well-known, respected and honored member of the community. Anne Arundel County "Man of The Year, 2008."

And Wayne Foltz? Well...he was ...a what? Carpenter? Glorified handyman?

More people knew Joanna and the kids better than Wayne. Yet, from the beginning, Tom knew he was the man needed to lead them. He was prescient enough to see where world events were headed and to take action accordingly. Wayne spent years and a small fortune accumulating his arsenal that provided them with the majority of their firepower plus body armor and military-grade night-vision equipment. As a former police commander he knew instinctively much of what he acquired had to be through less-than-legal means in order to avoid police and ATF scrutiny. Then there were the stockpiles of food basics which he shared with his neighbors most in need. He was the glue that kept the community together.

As for coordinating and leading the self-defense effort, he was more qualified for the task than Tom or even Doug for that matter. War experience? Grenada? Please. Operation Urgent Fury was little more than a glorified field exercise. Tom doubted he fired more than a dozen rounds during the action. His major claim to fame was the photograph of him being kissed by a rescued female medical student that was splashed on the front pages of newspapers around the world. Doug? He fought Desert Storm from the interior of an Abrams tank and never engaged the Iraqis from less than half a mile.

Wayne spent 19 months on the ground in Vietnam, slugging it out face-to-face against a ruthless, determined and merciless foe. In a conflict that highlighted body counts, his prime directive as a leader was to direct his forces to kill as many enemy combatants as possible. He had not been restrained by the cancer of political correctness that hobbled…many times with deadly consequences…the troops in Iraq and Afghanistan. Even 40 plus years later, he was expertly schooled in the tactics, strategies and combat methods needed to give them a chance at survival. Most of all, Wayne had the burning hatred needed to match the enemy's appetite for destruction. It wasn't a hatred based on race, nationality or ideology. It was rooted in his fear of witnessing all he loved die. Tom initially had been shocked by Wayne's assassination of the MS-13 thug. The rest of that day, he was besieged by neighbors who asked…how could he let him get away with that?

How could he not? Tom finally answered. Well, he was an officer of the law, they countered. What law? He responded. The Law of the Jungle prevailed and Wayne Foltz possessed the instincts to administer it without the flinching hell of self-doubt, hindsight or remorse. Tom wasn't capable of such moral certitude. He had spent too many years in the Jungle of Political Compromise. He had maneuvered his rise to power by expertly balancing the contradictory demands of enforcing the law and maintaining civil order against issues posed by race, gender, criminal rights, civil rights, opportunistic lawmakers and defense attorneys, soft-headed judges, civilian review boards and all manner of self-anointed busybodies and doing so in such an expert fashion that every competing faction believed they had his ear and his sympathetic understanding.

Tom Barton was, ultimately, the consummate politician. And it was because of politicians that he found himself and his family in the greatest peril of their lives. Now enveloped in his emotional darkness, he again began bartering with God; gladly willing to sacrifice his life in exchange for his comrade's.

Thirty-Five

As Wayne and Bill moved into the multi-floor Tudor house, Doug and Jim slipped silently around the rear of their target; a spacious rancher. They would wait until they heard weapons fire, then storm in from the back, kill as many targets as possible and drive the rest out the front and into Tom and Alan's crossfire.

Doug nervously fingered the AK-47's safety. He had never participated in close arms combat. He didn't fear the killing but he participated in a war ruled by computers and technology; of Tomahawk missiles that could be delivered with eye-popping precision. He never knew how many enemy combatants he might have killed because he never came within shouting distance of any of them.

What he faced now was so "old school" He'd actually hear bullets ripping flesh, do his best to block out the screams, step and slip in blood and experience close-up the death of his enemies. And while he never feared for his safety during Desert Storm, he realized in these circumstances the odds of surviving were 50/50 at best. He suddenly was aware he was standing in the middle of a large, paved patio. At this time of year, it would have made an ideal gathering place for a neighborhood cookout and party. What a fucking waste, he thought. We all saw this coming but too many people denied it or hoped for a political miracle that would have forestalled it. Those that sounded the rhetorical alarm were dismissed as cranks, reactionaries or political malcontents. He never had any respect for the anti-war crowd; espousing the fantasy slogan, "Give Peace a Chance." The belief that war could be abolished was antithetical to all of human history. Alexander the Great, Julius Caesar, Attila the Hun, Genghis Khan, Napoleon, Hitler, Stalin, Mao…etc…they were the historical norm, not the exceptions. Whether this war was triggered by the Iranians, the North Koreans, Al-Qaeda, Hamas or some other lethal brew of renegade states and non-state organizations, there was nothing new here. The history of the world was written in blood; only the authors changed.

Thirty-Six

It was General George Patton who said "change your battle plan to fit the circumstances." Wayne cursed the fact he couldn't communicate with the others to relay what he found because it materially changed their battle plan. It wouldn't be enough to inflict casualties and leave. Now it was imperative that they kill everyone in the vicinity and destroy this weapons cache and any others they might find. He moved quickly back up the steps, maneuvered through the trash on the kitchen floor and rejoined Bill who had remained in the hallway. He leaned close to him and whispered, "no mercy, no prisoners" He then motioned Bill to follow him up the steps. At the top there were 4 doors. Wayne pondered which rooms to hit first, knowing that weapons fire would bring others out. He finally decided that he would strike at those in the master bedroom and leave Bill out in the hallway to cut down anyone who emerged from the other rooms.

Bill took a defensive firing position at the top of the stairs. Wayne hoped he was up to the task of wholesale killing. No other experience in the world could approximate the split-second decision making required in combat. Any confusion or hesitation most likely would result with both of them dead.

The master bedroom was at one end of the upstairs hallway. Through the goggles Wayne could see the door was opened slightly. He pushed it open enough to allow him to slip inside. His quick scan of the room revealed 8 to 10 bodies sprawled across mattresses on the floor. They all were sound asleep. Perfect, Wayne thought. And then he started.

Thirty-Seven

Ritchie Highway once was the major road between Annapolis and Baltimore. Since the 70s, it had lost that designation but remained one of the most heavily traveled thoroughfares in the region. Now, it was an abandoned strip of concrete. Josh and Joe and the other extraction team of Will Owens and Bob Canale drove in tandem with their lights off. What was once a brightly lit collection of gas stations, strip malls and fast food restaurants was now a dim wasteland.

Josh was stunned they could travel in total darkness almost without fear of collision. Those infrequent times they did spot approaching headlights, they scurried to the shoulder, pretending to be one of a long line of abandoned vehicles. They finally reached the rendezvous point behind a once busy office complex. From their vantage point, they could see approach routes from virtually every direction. Joe had talked about his concern that they might become engaged in combat. Josh craved that opportunity. Growing up on books and movies like "Lord of the Rings" and "Harry Potter", he had heard the phrase "forces of darkness" to the point of cliché. Now, he wanted to confront the Saurons and Valdemorts that had plunged the world into chaos. Unlike the villains of imagination and literature, this evil could be killed. No matter how it ended, Josh wanted to take an active role in striking back…to kill as many of the bastards as possible.

Thirty-Eight

Doug saw the flashes and heard the bursts from Wayne's AK-47. He motioned Jim to follow him. They kicked in the back door and stormed into the house. They found themselves in a family room with an open kitchen off to their right and beyond that the dining room. Doug began spraying the area with the AK. His goal was to bring the enemy to them instead of seeking them out. And, if they decided to flee out the front, they'd discover that was a mistake.

Finding cover, Jim shot off his own burst. Then, in the main hallway, shadowy figures appeared. Doug and Jim held fire, hoping to draw them closer. The figures hesitated then moved slowly in their direction. In the green glow of the goggles, Doug and Jim could see 4 men; all carrying weapons. They kept advancing until they entered the family room area. Before they could fan out, they were cut down. Doug and Jim peppered the prone bodies with another burst and moved into the hallway.

Thirty-Nine

After Wayne made quick work of everyone in the master bedroom, he fired a burst into the adjoining wall to rouse the people in the next room. They would rush the master bedroom and those who weren't cut down by Jim would be greeted by Wayne's sawed off shotgun. Bill watched the doors to the other bedrooms fly open. He didn't bother to count how many emerged. He just waited until the hallway was full. In the dark, they didn't seem like men just ghostly apparitions. This dissociation made it easy to kill them without hesitation. It was ghoulishly amusing to witness their terror and confusion

Wayne heard the AK's chatter and waited for anyone foolish enough to seek refuge in the master bedroom. As if on cue, the door opened slightly and Wayne discharged both barrels. The door shredded like balsa wood. Above the roar and clatter of weapons fire were the unmistakable sounds of men dying, trapped in the melee of the surprise attack without sufficient time to counter.

Bill moved back down the steps as he was being rushed by those panicking to escape the lethal crossfire. He was amazed they were caught without their weapons being within easy reach. Wayne had been correct in his assessment that they lived and moved about without fear of armed confrontation. Their machismo hubris proved to be their undoing. Bill only hoped they realized it in the instant before their death.

There were no sounds, no activity from anywhere within the house. Doug began to wonder if the 4 bodies they encountered in the back were all to be found. He began to doubt his tactical approach. If there were more combatants hiding in the different bedrooms, they probably were armed. What kept them from bursting out and attacking head on was the knowledge that the narrow hallway would give Doug and Jim the perfect kill zone. Finally, they heard movement. But it was coming from behind them.

"Holy shit," Tom exclaimed when he spotted armed men climbing out of rancher's bedroom windows and circling around to the rear. He grabbed Alan by the arm and they raced up the front lawn in an attempt to intercept them.

"Coming out," Wayne yelled. The hallway was littered with the dead. "Bill?"

"Down here."

"You OK?"

"I'm alive."

At first Wayne thought that an odd response until he recalled his Vietnam experiences. In a close encounter firefight it was an almost counter-intuitive sensation to realize you survived. Before he could share that insight, he heard the distant melody of multiple automatic weapons fire.

Forty

Doug didn't panic when he realized they had been outflanked but Jim froze. His hesitation resulted in his being wounded by the on-rushing enemy despite his body armor. Doug was able to halt their advance long enough to grab Jim by the collar and retreat into the dining room. Doug knocked over the dining room table and hutch to provide cover. It would only buy them some time but not save them.

"How bad are you hit?"

"Left shoulder…arm. The vest stopped a few rounds but my ribs feel broken."

Doug helped him to a sitting position and gave him a revolver. "It's not much, but it'll have to do."

They heard shuffling sounds beyond their makeshift barricade. Doug raised the AK in the air and fired blindly. He waited for return fire. Instead they heard the sound of metal rolling across the floor. In an instant flash of recognition Doug threw himself on top of Jim as the ear-splitting blast turned wood, glass and press board into near lethal projectiles.

Tom and Alan arrived at the back of the rancher the same moment as Wayne and Bill, and only a split second before the explosion inside the house. "Alan, Bill…go around the front and be ready," Wayne instructed. He motioned Tom to follow him through the back door.

Particle dust and the smell of burning wood, sulfur and cordite hung in the air. Wayne hadn't given him instructions but Tom knew the mission was to kill anything that moved. No hesitation. No mercy. No regrets. It felt liberating. They could hear yelling in Spanish coming from the next room. Wayne didn't hesitate. He moved quickly towards those sounds and began firing. Instead of following him directly, Tom swung around in the opposite direction to blast them from the other angle. The crossfire produced screaming, hysteria and an out-of-phase synchronistic percussion from the AKs. Tom couldn't tell if anyone was firing back and later he'd feel foolish realizing he remained totally upright through the entire action. There was the crashing of glass and splintering of wood which indicated survivors were attempting to escape via the windows. Tom fired in that direction. Soon the only sounds came from the AKs. He and Wayne stopped firing...only to hear sounds of combat coming from outside.

Forty-One

Alan became increasingly anxious as he listened to the carnage happening inside. He had come to fight, to avenge himself but now he wondered if he had the stomach needed to face death while causing it. He wanted to ask Bill what had happened inside his old home but the sight of bodies pouring out of windows forced him to temporarily table his inquiry. Bill fired at the emerging enemy, startling Alan into a similar response. He feared they would turn and charge, they instead fled in the opposite direction.

Bill gave chase, firing off repeated quick bursts. Alan stopped, thinking he heard fire coming from some distance. He turned to discover enemy combatants rushing from across the street and up the sloped front lawn. Alan instinctively dropped to the ground. He tempered his urge to fire immediately instead waiting for them to advance on his position. Any fear he had felt vanished the instant he pulled the trigger. Instead he recalled the terror, destruction and death they had visited on this once-quiet neighborhood. The lives they destroyed, the joy they exhibited in their relentless cruelty. He felt elation as he watched one after another fall. From behind came the welcomed sounds of more weapons fire. The firepower from Wayne and Tom caused the enemy to reverse their head long rush. They broke ranks and began retreating.

"After them," he heard Wayne yell. "We can't let them escape."

Alan sprang off the ground and gleefully joined the chase. Cowardly motherfuckers, he thought; so easy to terrorize the helpless. Did you think we'd never fight back? He wanted to torture them, the way they had tortured him and his neighbors. But for now he was content merely to kill them.

Bill was angry that some of those he had pursued eluded him. While

84

he scored several sure kills, the others had split up and disappeared in the maze of houses and backyards. He rejoined the others just as they were coming back from their own chase.

"I didn't get them all," he reported.

"We didn't either," Wayne added. "I'm sure they're on their way to alert their friends." The aftermath of what that would mean was lost in the more immediate need to learn the fate of Doug and Jim. Their flashlights revealed that the explosion caused by the grenade had covered them with debris that they removed carefully. Doug was still on top of Jim. They both were alive but wounded. Wayne slowly rolled Doug onto his back

"How bad are you hurt?"

His eyes fluttered open. "Well, I know I ain't dead, because you're certainly no angel. I fucked up. I didn't secure our backside. They walked right in on us."

"Don't worry about it. We got most of them."

"Jim's unconscious but alive. He's a bit shot up but nothing vital was hit," Tom said. "We need to get them medical treatment. How we going to get them to the rendezvous?

"We can't worry about that now. We've got more important shit to do." Wayne then told them about the arsenal he discovered in the basement of Alan's home. "We'll help ourselves to whatever we can use. The rest we'll destroy by burning down the house. We need to check every house on this block for more weapons and we'll burn them too."

"What about the rendezvous? What about those waiting for us?"

Wayne checked his watch. It was a few minutes past 4am.

"Josh knows what to do."

Forty-Two

The night sky was beginning to lighten and as it did, it increased the dismay and agitation of the extraction team, except for Josh. He had been warned that few military actions go as originally laid out and had been trusted with contingency plans. It was time to implement them.

He called together the other three.

"It's obvious they've run into some problems. We're going to rescue them."

The three adults looked at each other, annoyed and offended at Josh's presumptive seizure of command.

"Who the fuck are you to give orders?" barked Will Owens. "We don't even know where they are?"

Josh didn't react or back down. He reached into his backpack and produced a hand-drawn map. He unfolded it on the SUV and illuminated it with his flashlight.

"My dad and Mr. Charles drew this up." He placed a finger at their ultimate destination. "It's about 10 miles up the road."

"Why'd they give it to you?" Bob Canale demanded to know.

"Dad was worried if you knew the mission could change, you might back out."

"Change? Oh that's fucking great!" Owens continued. "They could be dead."

"Until we know that for sure, this is now a rescue mission."

"Count me out," Joe Wiggins said.

"Fine," Josh countered still maintaining an icy cool that belied his age. "I'll go alone if I have to."

"You're as crazy as your old man," Bob Canale conceded, making it sound every bit like a compliment. "You act like you're not afraid to die."

"I don't want to die. No one wants to die! But when you go back down Ritchie Highway and see what a shit hole they've turned it into, ask yourself if you're ready to keep living the way we've been forced to live? Is that better than death? And if wasn't for my dad, Mr. Barton and Mr. McKenna where the hell would you be? They're certainly willing to die for us. So, what the fuck is wrong with you? This is not a time to cut and run."

"It's a hell of world when the biggest set of balls belongs to a 17-year-old." Owens finally conceded. "Let's go." No one hesitated.

Forty-Three

Wayne and Tom stood before the massive weapons cache in Alan's basement. They already had liberated enough automatic weapons, ammunition, 81mm mortars, grenade and rocket launchers to keep them well equipped for an even more prolonged siege, which now seemed inevitable. What was a bonus were the shoulder launched assault weapons that gave one man the firepower to stop armored vehicles or blast a small building to dust. What remained still inspired awe and fear. Now it all would be destroyed. The neighborhood already was aflame as the other homes had been set on fire. They would start the conflagration on the first floor and wait for it to consume the entire structure. This would allow them to finish loading and escape before the fire reached the munitions and set off a volcano-like eruption.

The rescue teams had arrived just at the conclusion of their most grim and odious task. They combed through the casualties seeking out those who were still alive and then executed them. No one protested killing the wounded and helpless. The goal of survival now made the once-unthinkable disturbingly routine. It was done quickly and without conversation or comment. What did promote discussion was that among the dead were many who obviously were from the Middle East. None carried any form of identification so they were left to speculate their countries of origin.

The sun was beginning to emerge from what seemed like the longest night any of them had ever experienced. Everyone stepped up the pace of activity because no one doubted those who escaped would be returning with more of their comrades. Wayne and Tom returned to the first floor. The air in the house was beginning to acquire a tinge of rotting flesh. As they had done previously, siphoned gasoline was the fire starter and accelerant. Once the flames began moving across the floor, they left quickly.

Outside they had created a version of hell that rivaled anything Dante or Bosch had put to paper or canvas. The dead littered the ground, unfit for last rites or burial. Homes up and down the street were totally aflame. Gas tanks exploded as make-shift wicks had been created to ignite lingering fuel and blow any useable vehicle into oblivion. The task of loading all the new firepower into the SUVs was near completion. The majority of weapons were placed in a Chevy Suburban. They "requisitioned" from among the enemy's vehicles a Cadillac Escalade and Land Rover which would be used to transport their wounded comrades and additional weapons.

Tom stopped to survey the carnage and destruction.

"I use to believe that this sort of thing could never happen in America. That no one…no country…would be foolish enough to risk attacking us on our own soil…to be able to do the things they've done to spread such misery and panic. Shit…we've been kicked back to the Dark Ages, just with better weapons."

The air roared with the sound of once half million dollar homes being transformed into gargantuan bonfires and in the distant background Wayne could hear the whine of engines. He looked at Tom whose nod acknowledged he heard it too.

Wayne quickly called everyone together. "We've got to get out now. Joe, you drive the Suburban, Bill, the Land Rover. Bob, you drive the Cadillac and take Josh and Will with you. Alan, you'll come with Tom and me in the Lexus."

By now, everyone heard the whine of engines and the danger it foretold. At the crest of the street appeared two military Hummers and a troop transport. They stopped.

"How the fuck are we going to get out of here?" Joe Wiggins muttered.

"You're going to drive up and over the embankment," Wayne told him. "Make straight for home and get them to Fareed. We'll try and hold them off so you can make your escape."

Tom could only stare at the force gathered at the top of the street. "How do you plan on doing that?"

"We're going to charge them."

"So now it's become Operation Charge of the Light Brigade?"

"It'll work. If we go right at them, they'll freeze. It'll give us a momentary advantage. You with me?'"

Tom nodded, "All the way."

"I'm going with you too," Josh said running up to Wayne. "You're going to need more firepower."

"You are absolutely determined to get me in serious trouble with your mother."

Will Owens was the next to speak up. "I'm coming too."

"You're volunteering for what could be a suicide mission."

"I got the balls to handle it." Will smiled and looked at Josh as he said it. Wayne wondered what was between them but this was no time to ask. He reached into the cargo bed of the Lexus, removed a rocket launcher and handed it to Tom.

"You're going to fire this when I give you the word."

"I don't know if I can figure out how this works!"

"You've got 30 seconds or we'll be totally fucked."

"How in the hell did you survive Vietnam?"

"Doing crazy shit like this helped."

Small arms fire erupted from the top of the street. They then saw the trailing smoke of a missile that veered wildly off course.

"Let's hit them before their aim improves." He looked back at Joe, Bob and Bill. "Go! Go! Go!"

The men gave the thumbs up signal, started their vehicles and drove cautiously up and over the steep embankment. Wayne hopped into the Lexus' driver seat. Tom, fumbling with the rocket launcher, took the passenger seat. Will busted out the sunroof while Josh and Alan climbed into the back. Wayne stomped the gas pedal, the Lexus jumped forward headed directly at the armed men at the top of the street. The SUV charging right at them caught them so by surprise they momentarily stopped firing.

"Now!" Wayne yelled. Will and Alan squeezed through the opening that once was the sunroof and began firing. Josh leaned out the back driver's side and did the same.

"The troop carrier! Hit the troop carrier!"

Tom had no confidence in his ability to hit anything but he pointed the business end of the launcher towards the carrier, gave a quick look through the sights and pulled the trigger. The rocket took off like it was on a string, passed between the two Hummers and struck the carrier directly in the engine block. It lifted off the ground and erupted in a burst of flames. Those still on board scrambled off to safety. Wayne turned hard left and steered the Lexus up one of the once fine lawns and between two homes, using them as shields against the eventual return fire. Gunmen climbed aboard the two Hummers and gave chase.

They flew between the two homes where the Lexus disappeared and failed to see it had pulled over and was tucked tightly against one of the homes. Wayne and Tom were positioned with shoulder launched assault missiles and took aim as the Hummers moved away from them. Wayne fired at the lead vehicle, Tom at the trailing Hummer. Tom scored a direct hit vaporizing his target. Wayne led his target too much. The missile destroyed the back of a house but the explosion caused the Hummer to lose control and crash into a tree.

"Fuck," Wayne yelled. Even though it suffered a major impact, the Hummer was not disabled. As it was backing away from the tree the ground and air groaned from the impact of a major explosion. The fire had reached the munitions stash.

"Damn, I really liked that house," Alan said from behind the wheel of the Lexus.

"This is your neighborhood. Get us out of here," Wayne instructed as he and Tom climbed in. Alan directed the nimble SUV on a vector designed to put as much distance as possible between the Lexus and the recovering Hummer. He steered it deftly avoiding large objects. The downside was that he was laying out a path for the Hummer to follow. The Hummer overran most fixed objects in its quest to overtake them. Alan used his knowledge of the area to zip between houses, cut through cul-de-sacs, backyards and play areas. But the Hummer could not be shaken.

The chase was devolving into a running gun battle. Every time the Hummer closed the gap, gunfire was exchanged but with no great consequence.

"We've got to lose him now," Wayne said. Alan nodded. Then Wayne saw on Alan's face an expression of delight, as if the perfect plan had just been hatched. He steered the Lexus onto the street and began to reduce speed. The Hummer rounded the corner and quickly caught up. Small weapons fire rattled the back of the Lexus. Will, Jason and Wayne returned fire but both vehicles seemed impervious to bullets.

Alan let the Hummer get perilously close before he accelerated and began to pull away again. Faster both vehicles went until Alan made a sharp right turn, hopped the curb and sped into a back yard. The Hummer followed, keeping pace with the Lexus' building speed. Alan had it aimed at a privacy fence fronted by a long, high hedge. Everyone braced for a collision but at the last possible moment, Alan jammed on the brakes and steered the Lexus away from a head-on impact. Its all-wheel-drive managed to keep the vehicle from spinning out of control. It swayed then fish tailed slightly, took out a section of hedge and fence and finally swerved to a stop. The Hummer, however, was too close and moving too fast to avoid a direct, head-on collision. It busted through the fence and the men in the Lexus hear the distinct sound of a watery crash.

Scrambling out of the vehicle, weapons at the ready, they found the Hummer nose down in the shallow, putrid water of a swimming pool. There wasn't enough water to drown anyone but no motion was detected. Wayne signaled Will, Jason and Alan to assume cover fire positions as he and Tom entered the pool from the shallow end.

They waded through waist deep water and approached the Hummer slowly and as they got closer they could see that its occupants either were dead or unconscious. They were, with one exception, Hispanic males. But that exception was a Middle Eastern male in full military uniform seated in the front passenger side.

"That looks like Iranian Army gear," Tom said. Tom shook him and he emitted a low moan. "He's alive."

"Then he's coming with us." He helped Tom extract him from the Hummer and carry him out of the pool.

"Let's get out of here before reinforcements arrive," Wayne ordered.

"What about the others in the Hummer?" Will asked.

"Kill them," was Wayne's simple command.

Forty-Four

Their return caused thankful relief in the community. The appearance and nature of the Captive caused alarm. It confirmed the unspoken suspicion that this war was rooted in a religious jihad that had gathered to it any faction that could profit from the collapse of America.

The Captive awoke to find himself bound tightly to a chair in what seemed to be the family room of a private home. What stirred him was the sound of a loud, shrill, chattering voice. When he regained total consciousness, his focus went to a small brunette woman excoriating a tall white male with flowing gray hair and a gray beard and a reed-thin African-American male. Other men in the room, all brandishing weapons, stood passively as the woman continued her endless torrent of words. Being American he understood everything and listened in silent amusement as she spoke of the Geneva Convention, war crimes, the UN Commission on Human Rights and the torture abuses of the Bush Administration. What patience these men have, he thought. He would have silenced her with a bullet.

The woman stormed out and slammed the door behind her. The men looked at each other, shrugged and laughed. He wondered what they planned to do to him. It didn't matter. He had spent years preparing for this moment. Born and raised in Rockville, MD, his parents had emigrated from Lebanon. His father founded a successful software development company and his mother was an attorney specializing in immigration law.

The turning point of his life occurred in middle school when he accompanied his Uncle Asif to attend religious services at the Dar al-Hijra Mosque in the northern Virginia suburbs of Washington, DC. Unlike his parents Uncle Asif was a devout Muslim; uncorrupted by the excesses of Western materialism. It was there at this Mosque that the Captive received and accepted the words of the Prophet and his command to make Islam ascendant over the entire world. Uncle Asif was part of an expanding group of scholarly Muslims who met regularly at the Mosque and railed endlessly against Western Civilization and its many crimes against the Islamic world. The Captive found the certainty and order of being a devout Muslim comforting and a much needed personal bulwark to withstand what he increasingly viewed as the moral cesspool of modern America culture.

The Captive often entreated Uncle Asif to come to his house but he refused. He condemned his brother and sister-in-law as apostates. Drawn deeper into the ideology of his uncle and his cabal of fire-breathing Islamists, the Captive was prepared to fully surrender his life to the Koran, The Prophet and Allah and to live inwardly and outwardly as a true believer. But Uncle Asif proposed a different game plan.

Uncle Asif viewed his nephew's conversation as just a preliminary step in a divinely guided plan. He instructed the Captive to keep Islam in his heart but to maintain the outward appearances of a typical American pre-teen. It was important to the future of their struggle that the Captive live among the Kafir as one of them. To become fully familiar in their ways would enable him at some future date to use that acknowledge against them in service to Allah.

The Captive protested that to live such a wretched existence convincingly meant not following key instructions of the Koran needed for him to achieve a life of righteousness. Uncle Asif reminded him that the Koran clearly instructed the faithful if victory over the Kafir required lies and deception then it was not just sanctioned but encouraged. Those whose actions contributed to the triumph of Islam would incur no divine sanctions or penalty.

And so the Captive began his service to Allah in the midst of the non-believers. Despite the conflicting emotions he experienced, he heeded his uncle's words. He came to pity then despise his family. He blamed his parents for not instructing their children in the words of the Koran and the ways of the Prophet. They had been totally co-opted by Western materialism, freely associating and cooperating with those forces in business and government responsible for repressing Muslims worldwide and contributing to their misery and poverty. His older sister he regarded as a self-absorbed, painted whore; prattling endlessly about boys, music, parties, shopping and clothes. He prayed daily that they would discover the true path before the time of divine reckoning.

He continued to surreptitiously attend services and lectures at the Mosque which increased his religious fervor. With each meeting he found himself among more young men of like mind, determined to strike a blow for Islam, to lash out at the oppressors. Uncle Asif and the other adult men at the Mosque cautioned them to rein in their anger and remain patient. Their time was approaching.

The Captive had barely begun his senior year at Richard Montgomery High when the moment arrived. He marveled in quiet jubilation at the destruction of the World Trade Center Twin Towers and attack on the Pentagon. When school was dismissed early he drove to the Dar al-Hijra Mosque. There he joined in a fervent celebration in honor of the glory Osama bin Laden had wrought in the name of Islam. He learned that several of the hijackers had attended services at the Mosque and received spiritual and material support. This knowledge coupled with repeated showings of the towers' collapse filled the Captive with pride and an exhilaration he never experienced. He told Uncle Asif he was ready to be a warrior for the faith as had the 19 heroes of September 11, 2001. Uncle Asif hugged him and whispered just one word, "Soon."

When he returned home he found his family distressed and in mourning over the justice that had been delivered in Allah's name. The Captive came to the full realization they viewed themselves as Americans first. Soon, they would be useless to him. He needed to maintain the charade until he graduated and he had become an expert in concealing his true self from others. Uncle Asif had been correct about them. They were Kafirs and when Islam and Sharia eventually swept across the diseased and corrupt beast known as America, they either would submit or he personally would put them to the sword.

Forty-Five

As a high school graduation present, the Captive asked for the opportunity to travel to Lebanon. He said, ostensibly, that he finally wanted to meet his Lebanese relatives and reconnect with his roots.

His parents were reluctant to honor this request so soon after 9/11. But he graduated with honors and in the fall would be attending the University of Maryland, majoring in engineering. In light of such accomplishments, they found it impossible to deny him.

Arriving in Beirut, he was greeted warmly by a collection of aunts, uncles and cousins. He barely would remember their names and faces because after one week he excused himself from his so-called homecoming, claiming he desired to travel to other parts of Lebanon and then Egypt. He ignored their protests and, much to their dismay and confusion, struck out for his additional "travels" in the middle of the night.

Uncle Asif had arranged for his nephew to be picked up at a pre-designated point and taken to Lebanon's Bakka Valley where, under the supervision and guidance of Hamas and the Iranian Revolutionary Guard, he began his training.

Although there were brother warriors from Europe and the Arab world, the Captive was encouraged by the number of American Muslims in attendance. He adapted rapidly to weapons training and urban guerilla tactics. Most of all, he totally absorbed the religious teachings that informed the call to jihad.

When he returned to America, he moved all of his possessions out of the family home to an apartment near the university campus. By now his transformation was apparent to those once close to him. His father's demand that he account for his time overseas was met with venomous scorn. In the blessed solitude of his apartment, which was financed by the Dar al-Hijra Mosque, he enjoyed the freedom to pray as required and communicated with his fellow American jihadists via coded emails.

He excelled at his studies but kept himself apart from other students. He attended meetings of the Muslim Student Council and the on-campus Muslim Student Center. He observed but never participated in any events or demonstrations. He had been cautioned to avoid anti-Israel or pro-Palestinian protests because it would be counter-productive to show up on any law enforcement agency's watch list. Anonymity was his strength. Besides, he found their efforts amateurish. Good intentions were mistaken for passion. Shouting down those they opposed or walking around with placards were weak substitutes for bold and decisive action. He did, however, manage to convince some of the young men to attend his Mosque where several fell under the sway of his uncle.

And every summer he returned to the Bakka Valley. And every summer he became a more skilled and more deadly fighter. And every summer his network of American-born jihadists grew. The invasion and occupation of Iraq motivated more young Muslims to join the Crusade against the forces of the infidels.

Finally, in the spring of 2006 the Captive celebrated two milestone events. He received a BS degree in mechanical engineering from the University of Maryland and later that summer, he was made an officer in the Iranian Revolutionary Guard.

Forty-Six

For the next three years he worked at a Washington, DC engineering firm. He strove to be pleasant and professional. Around the office he was known as a team player. Although he was viewed as quiet, even mysterious, nothing in his professional life gave rise to any suspicions. In early 2009 he received his first orders. He was given contact information for the individuals who would comprise the cell he would command. He also reached out, as ordered, to elements of MS-13 in the Maryland and Virginia suburbs of Washington, DC. It wasn't hard to persuade their leadership that it would be immensely profitable to go from a regional to national stage. He had his misgivings about their level of discipline but he had no question about their ability to inflict damage. They could be molded and once under his command, they'd be relentlessly lethal. Time passed slowly but he knew that patience would be its own reward. They had waged war against the non-believers since the 8th Century and now he sensed they were closer than ever to the arrival of the Mahdi.

The first attack command came via coded email. At that moment he knew nuclear warheads were on their way to Tel Aviv, Haifa and other targets inside Israel. They were launched as part of a pre-emptive strike. The Iranian government received reliable information that the IDF was on the brink of striking Iran's nuclear installations. Having Muslims in key positions at the highest levels of the Obama administration and in the Pentagon had beneficial consequences.

His targets were as general as the Washington, DC metro system and as specific as the homes of Senators, Congressmen and other members of the Washington political elite. They inflicted massive civilian casualties and even attacked several military bases. Those attacks were not successful from a military stand point but in terms of public relations, they were major victories. Reports of those attacks contributed to civilian panic and the perception the US military was rendered impotent.

They then melted back into the general population taking full advantage of the fact that hostile military actions were popping up all over the globe and the hunt for domestic terrorists became the primary responsibility of overworked and understaffed police departments. According to the original plan, once the United States launched retaliatory attacks and came to the aid of Israel, he would receive additional instructions on spreading more domestic chaos. Then the unimaginable happened. There were no immediate counter attacks. At first, he thought it was merely a strategic feint then with each passing day it became numbingly apparent that the executive branch of United State's government lacked the will to fight back. Instead, while American cities smoldered and thousands of Israelis perished, the President called for calm and an emergency meeting of the United Nations' Security Council. The news and cable stations crackled 24/7 with one overriding question...why hasn't the President of the United States acted to defend the country?

Into this void came the second wave of attacks. It was aimed at the West's communications network and energy grids using electromagnetic pulse bombs and cyber experts hacking into and disabling power grids. It was as if every electronic and mechanical device and system throughout the country was attached to one massive plug that suddenly had been pulled.

This was the next signal to move quickly, ruthlessly and decisively. They attacked police stations, conducted massive neighborhood raids and reigns of terror. With communications capability steadily deteriorating it grew impossible for law enforcement to pinpoint their movements. Resistance slowly crumbled. His cadre grew with every success. The well-off civilian populations in suburban Maryland proved easy pickings. He wasn't prepared when a command contingent from the Iranian Revolutionary Guard arrived and put a temporary halt to their rampage. Not that they were dissatisfied and disappointed with what he had accomplished. To the contrary, they were thrilled with his accomplishments. They would substantially upgrade his arsenal and reinforce his troops with experienced fighters from the IRG and Hamas. He received a field promotion to Captain and was ordered to wear an army combat uniform. He had gone from terrorist to one chosen to be part of God's holy mission to humble the Great Satan. The moment of his glorious triumph was near. A few more days and his forces would be unleashed to devastate and subjugate the civilian population. Many had fled their homes and neighborhoods but that would provide only a temporary reprieve. They would be found and used as pawns to force the arrogant and morally bankrupt American empire to acquiesce to a re-ordered geo-political reality.

He had been assured he would play an important role in this re-made America. He had lived his life as a citizen so he was an ideal candidate to assume a position of real power in what was once his native country. He found it amazing and helpful that over the last decade or more, the country's political elite had reoriented America's political direction to propagate a diminished role for America in world affairs. American exceptionalism, power projection and hegemony became hoary old concepts reduced to historical footnotes.

This was the path he had set for himself. He was Rafik Abdul Salim. Soon his name would be legend; inspiring fear from his enemies and adulation from his followers. But first things first. He would see to it that the fools in this room would pay for being a minor obstacle in this rise to power.

Forty-Seven

The big graybeard approached and extended a canteen.

"Thirsty?"

Yes, he was very thirsty but he feared he would be the victim of a trick. The graybeard took a swig from the canteen.

"It's just water...OK?"

Rafik nodded and Wayne pushed his head back and slowly poured refreshing water down his parched throat.

"And I know you speak English. When that mouthy bitch was going off on me, I caught you smiling in spite of yourself. You knew exactly what she was saying."

Again, against his will, Rafik smiled. His instincts told him that this old man planned and lead the daring attack that temporarily delayed his march to total victory.

Wayne offered him more water, which he accepted.

"You need a better poker face to be an effective commander."

"I suspect you know all about that, don't you?"

Rafik was pleased to see the stunned looks on the faces of his captors, except for the graybeard. He didn't appear to be a bit surprised.

"You speak English without an accent," Alan said in amazement.

Rafik smiled even more as the men's expressions grew darker as they realized the truth behind the person strapped to the metal chair.

"Would you feel better if I sounded like someone who worked at a 7-11?"

"You're an American. How can you be part of this? How could you do this to other Americans?"

"Some quests transcend borders, cultures and nationalities."

Wayne looked at everyone else in the room. Their anger was visible, palatable and rising.

"Tom, it's time to patrol the neighborhood." Tom nodded, knowing the situation needed immediate defusing. He herded everyone out of the room.

"So, now there are no witnesses," Rafik said with a sneer.

"Don't get your mufti in a wad. I had to get them out of here before someone took a shot at you. We've been hanging by a thread for months. No utilities, scrounging for food, no running water. People have no way of knowing what's happened to families, relatives, loved ones. Killing you might make them feel a little bit better."

"And you have no plans for me?"

"No…now I'm thinking I should have killed you with the others in the Hummer."

"Why didn't you?"

"I guess it was the uniform."

Wayne pulled up a chair directly across from his captive.

"You don't seem particularly shocked to find out I once was an American."

"Shit, that stopped being news years ago. It was no secret that young men like you were joining up with terrorist groups. The real problem is that our leaders developed a bad habit of not squarely confronting the truth about why it was happening and what it would mean. Tell me something, have you ever encountered a moderate Muslim?"

Rafik actually laughed. This man was knowledgeable which made him formidable. He finally met an adversary with the capability of causing him real trouble.

"How many units like yours are out there?"

He shrugged. "Enough."

"Those guys we whacked, the shit we blew up…all yours?"

"Yes!" Rafik said in calm anger. "Did you organize and command the operation?"

"I had a lot of help."

"It was brilliantly conceived and executed. Take no prisoners, destroy the arms and reduce the area to ashes rendering it useless. How did you find it?"

Wayne told him of the encounters with the two different groups of gangbangers and their subsequent fate and the value of the information derived from the notebook.

"That's the big problem with them. They're greedy and criminally inclined so they often freelance instead of following orders. The first two were on a reconnaissance mission, looking for pockets of resistance...like you. But they're children. They saw the shiny Lexus and decided they had to have it. The second group was sent to find out what happened to the first. I even sent my aide, Naser, to make sure they followed orders. When they attacked you, they were acting on their own in disobedience of my direct orders. Their stupidity cost the lives of 40 to 50 soldiers and all those weapons."

"Plus they don't seem to be the types who'd embrace the Caliphate."

"Their usefulness is only for the short term. Right now we channel their hatred of Anglos and niggers to our advantage."

"How did you manage to escape detection by the FBI?"

Rafik chuckled the way one would when knowing a truth no one else knows or could even imagine.

"It's the classic magician's move. Keep people's attention focused on your right hand while your left hand is performing the trick. Those busts of terrorist activity in Brooklyn, Chicago, Dallas....they all were set-ups. Our brothers were unwitting stooges. The operations were compromised by our own people as a way to lull the FBI and the public into complacency."

"Why are you telling me all this?"

"You're a brave and clever man and I respect you...the way one warrior should respect another. But I want you to know that everything you've done ultimately will make no difference. Unless you surrender to me and submit to the will of Allah, you will die; your family will die as will everyone who opposes us."

Wayne stood up slowly, glaring at his adversary. Based on his past actions, Rafik was sure he would be killed on the spot but Wayne left without uttering a sound.

Forty-Eight

Wayne immediately sought out Tom and impressed upon him the urgent need to gather together everyone remaining in the community for an emergency meeting. He did not doubt one word the American traitor had spoken. Somewhere nearby was that major armed force. It was seeking out their location with the intent of mass slaughter. Tom rallied everyone to gather in the community meeting room. People were frightfully restless wanting to know what knowledge had been extracted from the Captive. Wayne finally addressed the gathering, revealing what he had learned from the journal and the Captive and what he expected in terms of future danger. There arose from certain factions in the room a chorus of anger directed at Wayne and Tom and the others who had taken part in the attack from the previous night.

"This is your fault," shouted Patrick Hearn. Josh looked for his friend, Randy. Their eyes met and Josh could see he was embarrassed by his father's outburst.

"You guys had to go out and play solider, relive your glory years and be big heroes. Now we're all in real danger," Hearn continued. "Is this your idea of keeping us safe? If so, thanks for nothing."

There was a smattering of applause and shouts of support and agreement.

"I don't know what you have planned, but I'm taking my family and getting the hell out of here. Who's with me?"

This prompted even more applause. Hearn peeled off from the crowd followed by his wife and children. Josh noticed that Randy kept his head down, eyes glued to the floor. Other families began separating themselves from the gathering. They were, everyone would later observe, those always most resistant and critical of the self-defense effort.

"You're making a serious mistake," Wayne said, addressing Hearn.

"You know, I keep wondering who in the hell made you king? Who gave you the right to tell the rest of us how to act in this situation? We've listened to you and right now you expect us to sit by and just wait for Armageddon. Well, I'm getting my family out of harm's way."

Hearn's outburst caused more applause from those determined to follow his lead.

"You've always been free to leave. But you don't know what's out there."

"But I do know what's going to happen here and it's not good."

"He's right, don't do this," Alan broke in. "No matter which direction you go, you won't get 15 miles before you run into those animals. I've seen what they do to innocent people…women and children."

Hearn hesitated. He could feel the seriousness Alan radiated but he had gone past that point of no return. He left the room, his family followed as did several other families.

"God have mercy on them, "Alan whispered as the doors swung shut.

Forty-Nine

Silence draped the gathering like a smothering fog as they absorbed what had just happened. Wayne turned towards his neighbors. How many were crowded into this room? Perhaps it was 200…250…out of a community that once had over 1,000 residents. Had they stayed because they believed they would be protected and survive? Suddenly he felt this crushing weight squeeze him from all sides. Had he miscalculated and brought destruction upon them? He spoke and told the assembled that he would accept any role the majority prescribed. Tom spoke next, saying that he had complete faith in Wayne. But the most compelling and passionate testimony came from Alan, Bill Griffith and the others who had taken part in the previous night's raid. When they finished, a rolling wave of applause eventually filled the room. Wayne surveyed the crowd. So many of them he barely knew a few short months ago and now they all were bound by a mutual destiny. He had been a field commander in Vietnam, responsible for the lives of others but this time, as he looked into the faces of women and children he knew the stakes were immeasurably higher. And not just for them but for others who might suffer in the future if this enemy wasn't stopped.

Then, from the back, he spotted Emily. She was blowing kisses in his direction while being held aloft by Cindy and Alison. Wayne engaged in that physical struggle that all men experience when they refuse to become emotionally overwhelmed in public. Watching his granddaughter, daughter and daughter-in-law the task that lay before him was as plain now as it ever had been. They would not retreat. They would not lose. As the applause continued, Tom saw his friend fighting back tears. Unafraid of his own new-found emotions, Tom embraced him with a bear-like hug.

"It's OK, man. We'll win. With God's help, we'll find a way to win."

Fifty

As the platoon approached the village the soldiers instinctively began to fan out. It was the type of mission Wayne hated. There were reports of NVA activity so he was ordered to investigate. This sort of action could have only two possible conclusions. It would either be a boring waste of time or they'd be caught in an ambush. Wayne had little doubt which outcome they were facing. He brought their march to a halt. The village shimmered mirage-like in the brutal heat of late September as he gave his fellow soldiers a visual once over. Half of them were short-timers; less than 60 days left in country. Their faces showed the weary resignation of those who feared Death would be given another opportunity to snatch them. The rest were cherries...new replacements with little to no combat experience. Their faces were simply coated in abject fear.

That village had no strategic value. There was no fucking reason in the world for them to be out there. Except that some newly minted Captain at company HQ was looking to shine his superiors in a quest for another gold bar.

"Sgt. Wilborn?"

"Sir?"

"Sgt...what do you see out there?"

Armondo Wilborn of Port Arthur, Texas had been his non-com for almost a year. He was a massively-build African-American Wayne admired for his fearlessness. He wasn't quite a short timer but close enough that Wayne felt he deserved his special protection. Besides, he had provided Wayne with hours of entertainment describing what it was like going through middle-school and high-school with Janis Joplin. That made him a national treasure.

Sgt. Wilborn looked at Wayne, trying to figure out the point of his question.

"Sir?"

"What do you see out there, Sgt?"

As an ROTC student at the University of Iowa, Wayne had been mentored by Colonel Daniel Chapman, USMA '59; a highly-decorated veteran of two tours of Vietnam. A gangly and unsophisticated farm boy, Wayne felt awkward in his spit-and-polish presence. He worked hard to maintain his mentor's approval and often wondered why he seemed to prefer him over other students Wayne considered better qualified. After the commissioning ceremony prior to graduation, Colonel Chapman pulled Wayne aside.

"So, how does it feel to now be Lieutenant Foltz?"

"That fact hasn't really sunk in yet, Sir. I'm extremely grateful for your help and encouragement. I don't know what you saw in me but I'm glad you took an interest."

"Son, you make finishing at the head of your class sound like some happy accident. It's not. You're one of smartest and sharpest son-of-a-bitches I've ever met. But you also have one quality that showed me you're going to be a superior platoon leader."

Chapman's praise struck Wayne speechless, so he pressed on.

"You have a highly developed sense of responsibility to those under your command. It showed up in every psychological profile you took. In training camp last summer, your combat exercises showed time and time again your unwillingness to expose your men to reckless and unnecessary risks."

"I caught a lot of shit because of that, Sir."

"Yes, from the macho melon-heads in your class. Those shit-birds couldn't successfully lead a Cub Scout troop to the little boy's room. They're never going to find themselves in any critical leadership position as long as I have anything to say about it. I recommended you for a combat assignment because Vietnam is now the Lost Crusade. The Army desperately needs leaders who'll protect their men from the macho melon-heads that still can be found up and down the chain-of-command. They believe you should protect your men but only to the point where it doesn't interfere with their ability to pad their resumes at their…and your…expense."

"It sounds like the Colonel speaks from personal experience."

Chapman snorted.

"How do you think I ended up at this cow shit college? It was my career-ending punishment. But I get the last laugh, after all. I'm sending to my beloved Army the finest young officer I've ever had the privilege of knowing."

Colonel Chapman snapped to attention and saluted Wayne who was so stunned by this reversal of military protocol he hesitated before returning the salute.

"I know when the time comes you'll do the right thing and make me proud."

Wayne always wondered if the Colonel ever spotted the solitary tear that formed in the corner of his left eye.

"I'm still waiting for an answer, Sgt."

"I just see the village, Sir."

"Do you see any unusual activity?"

"I don't see any activity at all, Sir."

"Good, we've reached the same conclusion."

He ordered the platoon to reform ranks and ordered Sgt. Wilborn to lead them back to camp. A palatable sense of relief washed over the soldiers. During future unit reunions no one who was there that day ever spoke of what happened, not even to each other. It was if they feared speaking the truth would place their former leader in some form of jeopardy.

They needn't have been concerned because Lt. Foltz heard more than enough from a Captain John Joseph Marks at company HQ. His report of not finding any NVA presence at the village was not received graciously although Sgt. Wilborn corroborated every faux detail.

A scathing report from Captain Marks, accusing the Lieutenant of "engaging in a conspiracy of cowardice" was entered into his service record. He subsequently was re-assigned to desk duty, double checking and reconciling Quartermaster requisition forms. He realized his Army career was over but he didn't care. He had carried out the higher mission assigned to him by Colonel Chapman. During his desk jockey stint, which ended when he was re-assigned to Hawaii, he learned every short-timer who was out in the bush with him that day returned to the World safely.

Upon his discharge, he visited former-Sgt Wilborn in Port Arthur where he was given a grand Janis Joplin tour which concluded with their drunken duet of "Me and Bobby McGee" and "Mercedes Benz."

Fifty-One

Wayne spread out on a table an architect's scaled drawing of Chesapeake Heights. Its seclusion, even in times of rapid development, made it one the premier communities in the area. Wayne needed to turn these qualities into tactical advantages. Towards the end of the meeting, Wayne had been very emphatic about one unpleasant reality; people would be killed. This, he was sure, was why the others had fled. But those who remained didn't react negatively when Wayne put that fact out there. There were nods and grim looks but no arguments or complaints. He then designated Will Owens and Joe Wiggins to distribute arms and ammunition to anyone who needed them.

"Tom, what's your best guess on how big a force we're up against?"

"That punk we captured seems to be in his late 20s…early 30s, so he can't be more than a Captain in command of probably one Company. So, 200 fighters max."

"You know what bothers me? He was openly wearing an Iranian Army uniform. We already know from the Arab's journal they're planning on going from being a guerilla force to full-fledged occupiers. I think we're going to be hit with a small battalion force because they'll want to mop us up quickly and easily."

"Shit, that means we could be outnumbered at least 3 to 1," Doug added.

No one questioned Wayne's calculus of the potential combat situation. His focus was still on the drawings.

"How many grenades did we get from the raid?"

"A few hundred," Tom answered.

"Do you think we can get enough gasoline from the remaining cars to set the woods on fire?"

Those in the room began crowding around the table to get a clearer look at the drawings.

"They don't have air power and probably no artillery. There's only one road in and out of here," Wayne said, using his finger to run up and down that road as it was represented in the drawing. "They won't come down the road in any sort of force because it's only two narrow lanes and they know we have rockets and grenade launchers. To make sure, we'll block the entire road. So, their only option is to disperse and come at us through the woods on either side."

"You plan to booby trap the woods?" Doug asked.

"Right after they cross the bike and hiking trail." Again Wayne used his finger to point out the 25-foot wide ribbon of asphalt that cut through the woods from one end of the development to the other. "From the trail forward the woods are, what, just 75 yards deep on average? We'll rig trip lines tied to grenades and soak the immediate area with gas. The explosions will not only take a few of them out but it'll ignite the woods."

"We haven't had rain in weeks," Tom pointed out. "It's dry so it'll burn hot and fast. The woods run right up to some homes. The whole community could go up."

"If we set it up right and with some luck, we can take out a 25 percent of them before facing close combat."

Tom nodded. "We'll just live in tents then."

"OK, so someone sets off a grenade and the fire starts. What's to stop the rest of them from retreating to safety before they're trapped?" Doug asked.

"We'll have them surrounded. We'll have a force behind them and we'll keep them pinned in that section of the woods."

"Behind them? How in the hell are you going to get behind them without tipping them off?"

"We're going to become the Viet Cong."

Fifty-Two

Wayne worked quickly but carefully as he strategically placed hand grenade booby traps throughout the woods that rimmed the community. Underneath each grenade was a gasoline-soaked rag. He worried that it might not be enough to inflict the damage necessary to even the odds. So he added a few twists. He had sections of chain link, cyclone fencing and strands of barbed wire and concertina strung about waist high between trees along the outermost boundary of the woods.

The explosions and subsequent fire would drive the enemy forward and in the dark, many would find their escape blocked, some would be painfully cut on the wire. It all was designed to slow them down so that they would become easier targets. If it delayed their breakout from the woods even by mere seconds, Wayne estimated they enemy would lose an additional 20-25 fighters.

He also tapped into the community supply of propane tanks. He had distributed a majority of his cache so families could cook food on their barbeque grilles. Now, he reclaimed a number them to enhance enemy casualties. They were hoisted into the trees, positioned about 10-15 feet above ground, wedged where larger branches met the tree trunk. Once secured, they were camouflaged but not before spray painting a mark using florescent paint so they could be easily spotted using the night vision goggles.

On the other side of the hiking trail, Josh and others were busy excavating small underground bunkers. Wayne had given specific guidelines on how to proceed. It needed to be big enough to conceal two adults just below ground. It needed to be positioned facing the hiking trail and as close as possible to a big tree so the enemy would walk by it without much possibility of stepping directly on it.

Josh discovered that a big tree has big and extensive roots that made digging problematic. He refused to be discouraged. Their success depended on trapping the enemy so he had no choice but to make it work.

"How's it going?" Wayne called out as he approached.

Slow…you made digging this thing sound easy."

Wayne, carrying a shovel, pitched in to help.

"It's got to be done a certain way or else this will end up being our grave."

They placed the excavated dirt into buckets that was used to help build defensive firing walls on the other side of the woods.

"So, this is what you had to deal with when you were fighting in Vietnam?"

"Worse. The enemy had elaborate underground tunnel systems. They'd pop up, engage us in a firefight and literally disappear. They killed a lot of good soldiers…and friends."

"Have you ever stopped hating them?"

"It took awhile…but…yes. Why?"

"The prisoner…he's an American who decided it was his mission to kill other Americans….I think that's someone I could hate forever."

"Are you done with the grenades?" Tom asked as he approached.

"Yea…you can have them."

"And you're sure this will stop them?"

"It better, because if it doesn't…," with Josh within earshot Wayne decided to take a more positive direction. "It'll work. These terrorists…. they're trained for urban guerilla warfare…house-to-house fighting, ambushes. Our location and terrain gives us a huge advantage. They can only come at us from one direction. They'll send scout patrols through the woods looking for traps or ambushes before they attack. That's why I want lanterns lit at night along the picket line. The lights will be visible from the trail and I'm betting the enemy will stop because they don't want to reveal themselves. They'll go back and report we're only dug in across from the woods."

"There's another way they could come." Josh's statement caused both men to quickly turn in his direction.

"They could come down river and land on the beach."

"That's not only unlikely, it'd be foolish," Wayne countered. "They'd have to march through marshland and deep water. It would make them easy targets. Plus it's a manpower issue. We're spread thin already. We can't spare fighters to wait for an attack that probably won't come."

"That's why they'll do it because they know we're spread thin and wouldn't be expecting an attack from that direction. They only have to get a few to our rear to change the outcome. Besides, how tough is it to find boats in Annapolis?"

Fifty-Three

Chesapeake Heights was on the water, but not at the water. While many home owners enjoyed magnificent eagle-eye vistas, there was no natural water access of the type commonly found in other waterfront communities. As a result, the community beach was a totally man-made proposition. It was the creation of Dale Dunton, a politically well-connected developer and builder. He watched early sales languish as many potential buyers walked away due to lack of a beach. Even a complete pool and clubhouse complex failed to compensate for that lack of direct water access.

There was however, a narrow culvert carved out by rain water flowing down the bluffs into the bay. Being corrupt and pro-active, Dunton violated a host of local and state laws by dynamiting, excavating and bulldozing the culvert into a more level, paved and wider area leading to the water. Yet, this was only the prelude to an even bolder series of violations as he bulldozed, filled in and covered over protected marshland by trucking in tons of soft white sand.

To pay for his crimes, Dale Dunton merely increased his political contributions and gifts to the county commissioners, especially chief commissioner Ralph Alton. When the federal government finally caught up with Alton he, unlike then Governor Marvin Mandel, immediately pleaded guilty so as not to waste his accumulated financial gains on legal fees. As a result, Dunton was spared from the threat of exposure via the plea agreement between Alton and the feds. Yet, instead of using the Alton incident as a teachable moment, Dunton continued his extra-legal ways and was eventually hauled before the federal bar of justice for conspiring with Navy Commander Joseph Nolan to rig bids for work at the United States Naval Academy. He was sentenced to 12 years in a federal SuperMax facility where he died of multiple stab wounds inflicted by a fellow inmate unaware of his once lofty standing in the Anne Arundel County business and political communities.

Wayne, Josh and Will surveyed the community beach from one of the many bluffs that overlooked it. The beach actually was a sandy strip approximately 60 yards long and 30 yards deep. On either side, water sloshed against long stone bulkheads. Where the men stood was part of the recreational area with wooded picnic tables, and a small kids' playground.

"Josh, I'm telling you, a landing here makes no sense at all. Even if they get boats, the nearest launch site is at 3 miles upriver. And if they catch low tide, they'll be stuck at least 25 feet out in ankle deep mud."

"They'll do it because they'll want to repeat the first great modern victory of an Arab army and create their own legend of how they conquered the infidels."

"What exactly are you talking about?" Will wanted to know.

"In July 1917 an army of about 1,000 Arabs and Bedouins, lead by Lawrence of Arabia and tribal leader Auda Tayi crossed the Nafud Desert, 500 miles of sand and heat so brutal the Arabs called it "God's Anvil". They attacked the port town of Aqaba, which was occupied by the Turks. They did it that way because all of the town's defenses and big guns faced the Gulf of Aqaba. No military expert at the time could conceive that any force would be foolish enough to cross the Nafud where there was no shade or wells. But that was the only way to launch a successful surprise attack."

Wayne knew Josh had become fascinated by military tactics but his in-depth knowledge was surprising.

"General Grant here thinks we'd be making a major tactical error not covering the beach. He believes the enemy will anticipate that we'll leave it unguarded."

"And what do you think?"

"I'm worried about it now. I may have over thought the entire thing."

Will turned towards Josh, "You think they know this stuff as well as you do?"

"It was part of what was called the Arab Revolt. The goal was to end the rule of the Ottoman Turks and create a united Arab state. The Kafud crossing is part of Muslim folklore. The raid on Aqaba was the first victory for Arab army after being slaughtered by Turkish artillery at the gates of Medina. Ultimately, it led to their final victory and capture of Damascus."

Will shrugged. "I'm convinced."

"Recruit two others and be honest with them. You're going to be out here totally on your own. The rest of us are too far away to help. And if Josh is right, it's absolutely critical that they all die on the beach."

"Good, no pressure," Will said, flashing a rueful smile.

"Don't worry, they'll be sitting ducks. You'll be firing from above and they'll be crowded into moving up a narrow path. You'll get as much hardware as possible…grenades, launchers…and one of the BAR's we liberated from our friends. You'll be able to turn Aqaba into Thermopylae."

Fifty-Four

Wayne, Tom and Doug walked the community separately and together, checking on the final defensive preparations and looking for spots of vulnerability. They were examining the work done to build defensive firing walls when Alan, in an obvious state of extreme agitation came running up to them. He was serving as a lone sentry at the community entrance.

"There's an enemy patrol at the top of the road. They're waving a white flag. "They want to come in."

"How many?"

"I'm not sure. They pulled up in a transport and only the head guy got out."

"OK…get back and keep them there. He turned next to Tom as Alan ran off. "Tell the people working in the woods to stop and hide. Then round up some firepower and get up there, I'll meet you." But he saved his most important instruction for Doug. "Go get our guest. We might need him."

Wayne used hand signals to get those working on fortifications to stop and stay in place. He checked to make sure the chamber of his pump shotgun was fully loaded and then, at a brisk trot, went off to greet these unexpected visitors.

A half dozen armed men were already waiting for him as he reached the stanchions that marked the community entrance.

"Where's Alan?"

Joe Wiggins pointed down the road at the distant figures moving towards them.

"By himself???"

"He said he needed to make sure they didn't spot what was going on. Figured if he acted a bit over the top, they'd be distracted."

"Well, let's not leave him out there all alone."

They moved up the road, weapons at the ready even though the enemy was approaching under a white flag. Alan ran back to them.

"They've got hostages! They've got our people!"

"Our people?"

"The Hearns…the Millers….Pecoras…the people who left."

"All of them?"

Alan paused. "I don't know."

By now the entire patrol was within view. Like Alan said, those who had left were now prisoners. Their hands were tied and they were attached to each other by a rope at the waist. They stumbled forward in a ragged single file and there was visible evidence of abuse.

"Hispanic or Middle East?"

"They all look like Arabs to me," Alan answered.

"OK…everyone on guard. The white flag might be a trick. If you spot something that doesn't seem right…if one of them makes a wrong move… shoot to kill."

"What about the hostages?"

"We can't be concerned about them."

Tom arrived with reinforcements. Wayne quickly brought him up to speed. Accompanying the hostages was a force of six. One, who Wayne presumed was the officer in charge, wore a uniform similar to the Captive. The others were dressed in camouflage-style outfits.

The officer brought the column to a halt. "I want to speak with your commander." He spoke English without any trace of an accent.

"You can talk to me."

"We have captured your friends and neighbors and we want to strike a bargain."

"Go on."

"We'll exchange their lives for the surrender of your militia to our forces and acceptance of our authority."

Wayne felt a tap on his shoulder. He looked around to see Doug bringing the Captive. His hands were bound with duct tape and his head was covered with a cloth bag. Wayne motioned Doug to bring him forward.

"I'll tell you what, you treacherous piece of shit. Here's a counter offer." He ripped the bag from the Captive's head. The revelation evocated surprise from the other side.

"I see you know our guest of honor. I thought he should join our little party."

There began a conversation in Arabic between the Captive and his comrade.

"Boys! Boys! English please."

The conversation ended immediately.

"So here's the deal. You give us your hostages and we'll give you back your buddy, an even exchange."

The Captive again tried to communicate with his comrade. Wayne cocked his shotgun and placed it squarely in his back.

"I said…in English!"

"Don't bargain with him Khalid. I'm willing to be sacrificed. Stick to your demands."

Khalid walked over to one of the hostages and placed a pistol to her head. That it happened to be Monica Hastings struck Wayne as the ultimate cosmic irony.

"Either you agree to our terms or they'll all be killed."

"Go ahead. Be my guest. These people ran out on us. If you think I'm going to save their miserable lives and betray the people willing to stand and fight, then you're as stupid as you look."

Everyone knew that it wasn't a bluff. Khalid's eyes darted wildly as he attempted to comprehend how the situation had gotten out of his control. He cocked the revolver's hammer.

"I swear I will have them all killed."

"Alan!" Alan approached and Wayne handed him the shotgun. "Keep our guest covered and the instant you hear a gunshot, blow him in half."

"It'll be my distinct pleasure."

Wayne knew Alan would not hesitate. He would forever remember the malicious enjoyment Alan took in killing wounded combatants. He combed through the dead looking for survivors but instead of instantly dispatching them, he spent time gazing into their faces, in some cases talking to them. He was, Wayne decided, looking to identify his former tormentors. When he found one he went to great lengths to explain who he was and that he had returned to settle the score. Tom had implored him to get Alan to stop his macabre mission but Wayne let him continue because he was certain Alan also was killing his inner demons and once purged would become a more valuable combat asset.

Wayne removed a .44 caliber pistol from his waistband and approached Khalid and Monica. Khalid lowered his weapon.

"What's the matter, Khalid? Losing your nerve? Well, let me help you." His approach caused the others to train their weapons directly on him. On the other side; Tom, Alan, Doug and the rest stood ready for an old-fashioned shoot out.

Wayne placed his gun barrel directly on Monica's forehead.

"I'll kill them all myself. I'll start with her," he then swung his weapon and aimed it directly at Randy Hearn. "And then I'll do the kids. And if you try and stop me it'll get awfully messy because my friend over there will blast your comrade into little pieces and most likely you'll die too."

"Rafik?"

"He'll do it, Khalid. He's quite capable of it."

"Smart thinking…Rafik." Having finally discovered his name, Wayne pronounced it with a sneer. "You know, Khalid, it was awfully stupid just walking in here like you did without having an exit strategy or even a Plan B. Makes me feel like you have no respect for us even after we killed a lot of your buddies. Now, tell your men to lower their weapons and we'll make a nice quiet exchange and no one gets hurt."

Khalid motioned the others to stand down. When he did, Wayne lowered his revolver and walked back to his side.

"Go get them," he said quietly to Alan. "We'll cover you."

Everyone watched silently as Alan cut the prisoners' bonds. They were haggard, emotionally devastated and some became overwrought once freed. Other members of the community who had gathered to watch the latest confrontation went to their aid. They were confronted by weeping, wailing and hysteria. Several of the older children had to be physically restrained from attacking their former captors. Wayne had taken Alan's knife and was slowly cutting through the duct tape thickly wrapped around Rafik's wrists.

"You don't have enough fighters to prevent the destruction that Allah will bring down on you. If you surrender, at least your lives will be spared."

Wayne kept carefully cutting Rafik's bonds and spoke to him without looking up.

"I want you to go back and tell every cowardly traitor in your army that even if you defeat us, inevitably our God will smash your god. In the future he'll be nothing more than a historical afterthought…like the ancient pagan gods."

Now he looked at him eye-to-eye as he finished cutting the tape

"Tell them that the Mahdi will never set foot on American soil."

Rafik managed to break the final strands of the tape. He glared at Wayne as he massaged his wrists.

"But most of all, tell them I'm going prepare for our battle by wiping my ass with the Koran."

From his body language it seemed for a brief second that Rafik was prepared to lunge at him but he used his forward motion to step around Wayne and join Khalid's patrol.

"Alan, take 5 people and escort our guests out of here. Anything happens, you know what to do."

Rafik walked backwards all the way up the road, never losing sight of Wayne who made sure he remained highly visible.

"You don't have a copy of the Koran and even if you did you'd never... well...you know....," Tom observed.

"He doesn't know that. But his hatred will convince him that I would. So before the first shot is fired, we'll have a strategic edge."

Tom couldn't imagine what Wayne possibility meant but he had learned that as a commander, he always seemed to be several steps ahead of everyone else. When Alan and the others returned they turned back into the community to continue the work of preparing for battle. They hadn't gone more than a few feet when they were confronted by Monica Hastings. Wayne had always considered her attractive but now she seemed drained and lifeless; like some child's porcelain doll whose luster had been removed by neglect and abuse.

"You were going to kill me. I know you would have pulled the trigger. You would have killed all of us and not blink an eye."

When Wayne didn't reply to defend his actions, it left no doubt that he had been prepared to commit what normally would have been considered an unspeakable crime of mass murder. What troubled her even more deeply was that no one among the dozen or so assembled raised a voice of concern over the bloodbath that might have happened.

"Look at what you've all become. Now, you're as bad as they are."

"We can't afford not to be," was Wayne's soft-spoken reply.

Fifty-Five

Wayne was certain the attack would come within 24 hours. That quickly became the consensus throughout the community. Everyone worked at a quicker pace to build up their defensive positions. Wayne supervised the completion of the underground bunkers. Doug helped the different fire teams reinforce their positions and adjust their lines of fire. Tom distributed the remaining weapons, ammunition plus flares, grenades, grenade and rocket launchers. There would be nothing held in reserve.

Wayne was helping put the finishing touches on a bunker when he saw Tom approaching. His arms were extended in front of him and he was carrying something much in the way one would cradle and carry an infant.

As he got closer, Wayne saw it was the American flag that flew daily from the flag pole in front of the community center. In the ensuing months of chaos, its absence was never noticed. It was neatly folded in the prescribed manner and placed inside a transparent plastic bag."

"I found it in one of the storage rooms. I thought this might be a good time to break it out again."

The two men walked towards the community center with Tom still cradling the flag. Others fell silently in step behind them. When they reached the flag pole, Tom and Doug performed the flag raising ceremony with military precision.

"Remember after 9-11 you saw bumper stickers that said, 'these colors don't run'?" Tom said quietly to Wayne. "I only wish those motherfuckers could see her up there and realize we're not going to run either."

Wayne observed that all eyes were still focused on Old Glory as it unfurled and flapped in a quickening summer breeze.

"That doesn't matter," Wayne assured him. "We know she's up there. Right now, that's all that counts."

Fifty-Six

There were only a few hours of daylight left and Wayne knew that everything that could be done had been done. All that remained was to wait. Many had already assumed their posts. They did so quietly, purposefully without needless chatter. They were prepared to stay out this night, the next night or however many nights it took before they faced the enemy attack. Wayne suspected Rafik didn't possess the intuition to realize his victory would be assured if he delayed an attack for several days. The longer he waited, the more the morale of the defenders would drop. Right now, they were emotionally and psychologically ready. But after a few days their worry, fear and anxiety would mount. Their resolve would weaken and their courage ebb. Wayne was convinced that Rafik, blinded by religious-induced fury which he had deliberately exploited, would overlook that possibility. This battle had taken on the aura of a personal Holy War. Secure in his belief of a divinely mandated, pre-determined outcome he would not consider any other tactic but an immediate full-force attack. "And why not?" Wayne mused. They had vastly superior numbers plus they had extracted valuable information about the paltry numbers of defenders by torturing Patrick Hearn and other captives. More than anything, Rafik wanted personally to kill Wayne for the success of the raid and for his boast to defile the Muslim holy book.

Before he went home to check on his family, Wayne had one more stop he felt compelled to make. He had asked Alan to anchor what he considered the most critical defensive position. It was on the far right end of the picket line and overlooked where the woods curled in a fish hook pattern, thinned and allowed access to the first group of homes. Wayne was impressed with the construction of their defenses. Instead of a straight wall this one was horseshoe shape offering protection on three sides. Instead of being constructed entirely of packed earth they used patio pavers and bricks to fortify it. Alan was seated within the horse shoe. With him were Bill Griffith and Jim Barnes. He had handpicked them because of the way they had performed during the raid. They now had a taste for killing and wouldn't hesitate once the action started.

"Looks good," Wayne said as a greeting.

"Needs to be," Alan replied. Stashed in the horseshoe were an array of automatic weapons, rocket launchers, hand grenades, mortars and the other BAR. Alan patted one of the launchers. "We're loaded and ready."

"Walk with me."

They walked towards the fish hook without talking. They stopped when they got within a few feet.

"I've rigged so many booby traps in the fish hook no living thing can walk in there without setting them off. Hopefully it'll create a big enough killing field." Wayne looked back at the horseshoe. "You can't let them get around this flank. I don't care what you have to do but you have to keep them pinned down in those woods. The fire should help you out."

Alan scanned the growingly overcast skies. "Smells like rain."

Wayne nodded. "I'll see you when it's over."

They shook hands and Wayne started to leave.

"Wayne!"

"What?"

"Thanks."

"For what?"

"Just thanks."

Fifty-Seven

As he settled back in the horseshoe, Alan regretted he couldn't adequately explain his gesture of gratitude. He was grateful to the people of Chesapeake Heights who had given Laura and him shelter but most of all to Wayne for giving him the opportunity to strike back and relieve his deep shame.

Everyone knew the broad stroke details of the nightmare that engulfed them when their posh neighborhood was occupied by members of MS-13. What they didn't know was how Alan tried to appease them; he housed the leaders, fed them, give them information about his neighbors, lied to the police the only time the police were still capable of conducting any sort of investigation. He had become a quisling in the hope of somehow escaping the fate he was helping facilitate on those around him. He was the man who fed the crocodile in the fatalistic hope he'd be the last one eaten.

And when they finally did turn on him, they exhibited a malevolence he could never have anticipated. His cooperation only earned his captors' disgust who, despite the advantages he provided, viewed him as just another snitch. In their world that left him beneath contempt. While he did his best to stoically bear the daily humiliations and occasional beatings, it was the treatment Laura received that brutalized his soul beyond any redemption. That she was four months pregnant with an obvious baby bump did not spare her from being groped, fondled and physically abused just short of outright rape.

Her subsequent miscarriage seemed a foregone conclusion. It was at this point that Alan found the nerve and opportunity to make their escape. The thugs made it almost too easy, leaving them and their remaining neighbors alone while on a raiding expedition.

Wayne suspected they were allowed to escape because they had outlasted their usefulness except to spread fear and panic among the communities that would take them in. Although free from physical torment, Alan lived with constant psychological torture. His relationship with Laura was finished. It was not his inability to defend her that had built the unbreacheable wall but his sycophantic relationship with their captors.

They stayed initially with the McDowell family. He found it curious how they and others in their circle constantly derided Wayne. Although their first meeting was brief, Alan thought Wayne was a reasonable fellow and he totally agreed with the concept of community self defense. Besides, Tom Barton spoke very highly of him and Tom was one of his accounting firm's most valuable clients. He refrained from defending Wayne to his hosts for fear of seeming ungrateful. Yet day after day the sound of small arms fire coming from the Foltz backyard worked its sirens' song on him.

When he finally decided to investigate he was surprised at how many people were gathered at the impromptu firing range, waiting to be issued a weapon and to receive instruction and training. He was greeted warmly by Tom and Wayne personally showed him how to handle everything from a 9mm to a SR-15 and AR4. Alan's personal epiphany was that these people were not misguided or delusional but, instead, saw the direction of future events with crystal clarity. It was easy for Alan to decide in what camp he belonged. He thanked the McDowells for their hospitality and with Laura moved in with the McKennas.

Now he stared up at the sky as the atmosphere swirled with signs of an impending storm. How appropriate for this moment, he thought. He anticipated the coming battle with a sense of relief. His life was ruined but thanks to Wayne he would be able to prevent others from suffering his fate. He was ready to die and unafraid at the prospect. And for that more than anything, he was grateful.

Fifty-Eight

Josh buzzed through the community trying to re-connect with his friends. As part of the community defense plan families were relocated from isolated, outlying homes to homes located around the community center to make non-combatants more easily defendable if the enemy broke through. He helped Brittany Matthews and her mom settle in with the Griffiths but he had been unsuccessful in finding either Randy Hearn or Adam Pecora. They had avoided him and just about everyone else since their rescue. Despite the group's collective silence some details were known about their captivity and circumstances around it. Randy's father had been beaten, tortured and killed. Howard and Anne Snyder had been machine-gunned to death when they attempted to escape in their car. But the most abhorrent crime had been the sodomy and rape of Melissa Pecora.

The details were scant, as if not acknowledging them would effectively deny their reality. What was known was that she had been dragged into the back of a troop carrier and violated by an unknown number of men. The other captives were forced to listen to her screams and cries for help. Since her return, she had barricaded herself and Adam into their house, refusing all visitors and rebuffing all attempts at help and comfort.

He didn't find Randy, Randy found him. He asked Josh how he could be part of the coming fight. They were the same age but Josh viewed himself as the adult. From the outset Randy had treated the entire situation as an extension of some game…one in which he could determine his own level of participation. For Josh and his entire family, they were "all in" from the outset. But every willing fighter was desperately needed so Josh told Randy to find either Mr. Barton or Mr. McKenna and request an assignment. He then went off to continue his search for Adam.

He couldn't find anyone who had seen the Pecoras since people began changing residences. He checked at homes where he knew families were doubling up and still no sign or sighting of Adam or his mother.

With twilight approaching, Josh decided to check the Pecora home. Ms. Pecora had become a hermit so it made sense to Josh that she would refuse to leave even for safety reasons. He didn't know how he would persuade her to move but he'd give it his best effort. As he approached there were no signs of activity. He knocked, waited and then opened the front door. Josh stepped inside, stood still and just listened. He called out to anyone in the house. Silence was the only response and it was a silence that made Josh shudder. He took the safety off his weapon and began searching through the house.

The downstairs was unoccupied and Josh began a slow ascent up the stairs. He reached the second floor landing and instinctively walked towards Adam's room. The door was wide open and when Josh stepped inside he was not surprised or even shocked by what he found. Adam was in the bed, his head resting on a blood soaked pillow. His mother was sprawled on the floor at the foot of the bed. Near her right hand was the revolver Wayne had given Adam. He knew immediately that he would not reveal this discovery to anyone. It would serve no good purpose to alarm and upset the community at this moment with so much at stake. The sadness that should be expended over this tragedy would have to wait. Josh searched Adam's dresser until he found the box of ammunition then he picked up the revolver and tucked it into his waistband. There was a battle to be fought and every weapon and every round was needed.

Fifty-Nine

Joanna forced herself to look in a mirror. Generally, the women now avoided mirrors like vampires. She couldn't believe all the grey in her hair, the dull pallor of her skin and the overall gauntness in her face. Attention to feminine grooming, idle chatter and gossip were among the war's collateral damage. In a house full of women talk of men, dating, fashion, hair, make-up, nails and shopping was replaced by the topics of food rationing, finding water, bathing, personal hygiene, outdoor latrine and garbage ditches and their peculiar odors, clothes mending and treating illnesses.

Joanna became a combination of Earth Mother and Ma Barker in her work to maintain sanity and encourage optimism while upgrading weapons training. Her tasks were made easier by everyone's stoic acceptance of this new world order. It also helped that they were slightly better off thanks to Wayne's stockpiling of food, a supply of propane and a small generator. But even as they cut back and conserved, the food had been substantially drawn down by their own use and through sharing. The generator had been silent for weeks as gasoline became more precious and what remained had been diverted to combat-related uses.

As she watched Wayne and Josh perform weapons checks, she thought of Spartan women who sent their husbands and sons to battle with the admonishment that their only choices were victory or death. But those conflicts were fought on some distant battlefield. This one would come right to her front door. The disparity in numbers made that a near certainty. Joanna was ready and confident her daughters were too. She tried not to think about the alternative to victory. She already knew that no matter what action she had to take, no one in the house would be taken captive. Wayne approached her and held out his body armor.

"Think you can use this?"

"You're not going to wear it?"

"No one else out there will have this type of protection so I won't either."

That was so Wayne, she thought. They had only been dating a few months when she accompanied him to a reunion of his Army unit. Every man was happy to see him, praised and toasted his leadership. She was enthralled by their tales of combat and how light heartedly and comically they talked of their near brushes with death. What was obvious was their lasting affection for the man who had been their leader. Wayne was embarrassed by how they regaled her with stories of his combat skills, his devotion to the men in his command and the personal sense of loss he felt when a soldier became a casualty. And when they spoke of their departed comrades Joanna witnessed emotional and tearful declarations of love she never thought men could express.

When she returned to her cloistered academic world her colleagues reacted with a measured skepticism over her new-found enthusiasm for the man she openly declared as her "boyfriend." Wayne, in their estimation, was just a hillbilly who happened to luck out and attend college but not that it did him any good. He spent 4 years in the military after all, and what sort of person does that…unless they have no other options?

This elitism-fueled condensation became the first small tear in the fabric of Joanna's worldview. That they were wrong about this was only the first of many errors and distortions she discovered in her ersatz belief system.

She took the body armor from him. "It won't fit me. How about you, Josh?"

Josh shook his head. "It'll just get in my way."

What a man he's become, she thought, but under such brutal circumstances. She wondered if he would ever return to being the carefree, sometimes brain dead teenager from just a few short months back.

"OK," Wayne said. "It's time to move out."

Wayne looked around the room. All the women were there, looking at him. It was good he could see their faces. He'd carry the images with him so he wouldn't falter or stop opposing the invaders.

"Look out for him," Joanna said nodding towards Josh.

Wayne smiled. "He's proven he can take care of himself." That brought a smile to Josh's face.

"You know," Joanna started as she moved closer to her husband, "I've spent so much time trying to keep this place from collapsing, I've overlooked some important things."

"Like?"

"It's occurred to me that I can't remember the last time I told you how much I love you."

Everyone could see Wayne blush. "Well…uhhh….like they say, war is hell. Not much about that helps romance. But now that you mention it, I love you very much. I love you guys with all of my heart."

Joanna had hoped for a one-on-one hug but she would never regret that everyone gathered around them and amid some muffled sobs sent Wayne and Josh off to battle with a reminder of what was at stake.

Sixty

Tom hunkered down in his foxhole. His fire team was positioned where the woods on both sides ended at the road leading into the community. Their mission was to seal off both flanks and to keep the enemy bottled up in the woods as long as possible. The road had been blockaded along its entire course using furniture, scrap metal, jagged lumber, cars and SUVs including his beloved Mercedes Benz. It had a diesel engine and that fuel had been unobtainable since the conflict started so he didn't mind sacrificing it. Wayne joked that the gangbangers might hijack it instead of attacking.

What if all their assumptions were wrong? What if they arrived in heavily armored troop transports that could just smash through the roadblocks? They could pour into the community and overrun them before the members of the Bunker Brigade could scramble out of hiding to help them. What if the diversion was successful and they moved through the woods with mine detectors? Wouldn't the weapons of the men hidden in bunkers set them off? Even if the plan did work, they had only 91 men under arms. How many of them truly could be counted on to stand and fight? Tom's comrades at this post were Fareed's two sons, a dentist and administrator from the Department of Motor Vehicles. Amir and Hassen were eager for the fight but they were young and untested. Tom had requested they join him so he could, as much as possible, keep a watchful eye over them. Yet, would anyone be shocked if any, if not all, of his four compatriots, broke ranks in the face of enemy fire?

It seemed to Tom to be a stacked deck. So many things could go wrong and just a few twists of fate could spell their doom. Success would ride on an entire set of fortuitous circumstances aligning near perfectly in their favor. Wayne's plan made sense but it had a Rube Goldberg contrivance to it. Still, Tom had to admit it was far superior to any other plan offered. It was just a reflection of all the obstacles and shortcomings they had to acknowledge and plan around.

Josh had talked about how in the early stages of the Revolutionary War, homegrown militias regularly broke ranks and fled when confronted by the firepower of British regulars. Tom didn't find that particularly comforting. He settled down in the foxhole taking his turn at the watch while his fire team partners slept. Fuck it, he whispered to himself. Bring it on; we're going to kick your ass.

Sixty-One

Josh was glad he had lived the entire summer without air conditioning. Otherwise he couldn't imagine surviving in the stifling atmosphere of this small below ground bunker. Even though there was a steady breeze, the early warning of a late summer thunderstorm, none of that could reach him to provide any relief. He, like everyone else, had adjusted to a life of depravation. Discomfort caused by hunger, lack of regular bathing, lack of toilets, washing machines and refrigeration was a daily and accepted fact of life.

While Wayne dozed a few feet away, Josh strained to hear sounds above ground, especially footsteps. Every now and then he heard what he thought to be a clopping of hooves. Deer? Not likely. Once these woods were infested with deer but they had been hunted for food and essentially wiped out. Not a big loss in Josh's estimation. The big loss was domestic pets. They had become a major war casualty. Like most suburban communities, pets were an integral part of virtually every household. But as conditions deteriorated and food became scarce, pets became a liability especially dogs. When they began disappearing nothing much was said. Josh's sisters had a pet beagle named Rosie. She was a consummate scent hound, a nose with four legs attached. One morning, after they let her outside, she disappeared. Speculation was that that because there was no dog food and she was down to one small meal per day, she followed her nose in search of food. Or perhaps she had been snatched by a larger predator. It didn't change the outcome. Rosie was gone. Josh hoped she met a better fate than the other neighborhood dogs. Cats fared much better. The creation of garbage dumps in the community increased the vermin population which for cats was like opening a smorgasbord. Thinking of vermin gave Josh the shivers as he wondered what might be crawling around him in the dark. That thought had barely settled into his consciousness when it was jarred by a sound he was certain was a footfall.

He went to shake Wayne but he already was awake and intently listening. Wayne put a finger to his lips but Josh had no problem being silent. He even held his breath afraid the mere act of breathing would betray them. They remained motionless as the footfalls increased and moved closer.

Tom thought he had heard the sound of engines but before he could be certain it stopped. Now he could hear the enemy tromping through the woods. It seemed Wayne's plan was working. God help the men in hiding. Success rested squarely on their shoulders. If they could survive fear and claustrophobia and if the booby traps worked…if, if, if…the damnable unknown haunted every move. Tom looked at the dentist and administrator. They betrayed no nervousness or even fear. Maybe he had been worried for nothing. He knew Alan for years and he had, through force of will, transformed himself from an accountant to a fearless warrior. Perhaps there remained enough of the American spirit and love of liberty that motivated men to put aside their fears to fight and risk death rather than submit to slavery.

Scouts reported to Rafik that the road leading into the community was completely blocked. This didn't surprise him. If the road were open, he would expect to be attacked from either side of the woods. It was apparent the Old Infidel wanted to steer them into the woods most likely because it had been booby trapped.

He sent scouting parties into the woods as potential sacrifices. If they made sufficient penetration and returned without casualties then he would attack in full force through the woods. He saw no need to hold any fighters in reserve. It would be more than 300 men against their handful. What's more, Rafik had a surprise waiting planned for the defenders. He congratulated himself on his clever leadership. He had spoken of the magician's skill at diversion and he had made that part of his battle plan. While the defenders focused their attention to the front, they wouldn't be prepared for what would occur to the rear. Rafik wanted not to merely defeat them but to crush them and subjugate them to the authority of Allah. No matter how skilled a warrior, Rafik was certain the Blasphemer had never heard of the Siege of Aqaba.

Sixty-Two

The footfalls became louder. It sounded as if they were practically on top of them. Then they faded in the direction from which they came. Wayne was silently elated. Many had questioned why he limited the placement of grenade traps to the final 25 feet of woods, allowing the enemy to advance that far unimpeded. It was, he explained, the only way 90 fighters could successfully outflank and surround 300 enemy combatants.

The scouting parties reported to Rafik that the woods were clear. He paused before ordering the final attack. Surely, the Old Infidel was not relying on his numbers to defeat them. He had reviewed the inventory of the destroyed cache of weapons and even if they made off with 90% of what was there it could not compensate for their lack of force. It confounded him at first but he refused to let self doubt keep him from his destiny. He had circulated a description of the man who verbally defiled Islam and its Holy Book. He was to be captured alive and before the victors and any survivors Rafik, who believed himself God's messenger, would behead him for his insolence.

Soon, the footfalls returned but now they were quicker and so numerous they reverberated in their underground chamber. So confident was the enemy they did nothing to conceal their approach. They were making no effort at a sneak attack but thundering straight ahead. Then the air was pierced by the shrill war cry of the Bedouin and desert tribes plus they fired their weapons in the air as they advanced. Straight out of Lawrence of Arabia, Josh thought. Wayne gave him the thumbs up. At any moment their war-like cry would be interrupted by exploding metal and fire.

The Arab war cry startled Alan but his reaction was laughter. He got the BAR in final firing position while Bill and Jim trained their grenade launchers on the fishhook. They looked at each other and nodded.

"Company's coming," Alan said. "Let's give them a warm welcome."

With the noise of the attack, Tom realized they launched a full frontal assault. He alerted the others to take their firing positions. Tom hefted a rocket launcher on his shoulder. He smiled. He only regretted he couldn't see the look on the enemy's faces when they ran into the booby traps.

At the far northern side of the community the gently sloping landscape gave way to a massive outcropping of boulders. It was here that the woods and the ground diverged. At the top, one looked down on the woods as they fell away towards the Severn River. Doug and Joe Wiggins had settled atop the highest point to provide mortar support to the defenders below. Strategically it was the most advantageous position because they could direct fire on the woods yet remain secure because in the absence of artillery, it would take an all-out assault to dislodge them. Like everyone in the vicinity they heard the war cry and like every other defender, they would hold fire until the booby traps began doing their deadly work. The rolling, guttural sound and the firing of weapons were meant to intimidate them. Instead it inspired a promise to make that sound stick in their dead throats.

Sixty-Three

Few had any real concept of the sound made by exploding grenades. Most imagined there would be a solitary explosion followed in neat timely fashion by others, as if it were a collapsing domino exhibit. But as the enemy crossed the hiking trail and stormed into the canopy of trees closest to the community, their headlong rush caused a Chinese-fireworks effect. There was a string of near-simultaneous explosions accompanied by the screams of the dying and wounded.

On cue, the defenders poured on the weapons fire in their effort to turn their beloved woods into an arbor of death. Wayne, Josh and all those hidden burst from their bunkers to catch the enemy in a deadly crossfire.

Wayne drew a bead on the first propane tank that appeared in his night-vision goggles. He fired several shots that pierced the tank igniting a thunderous fireball that rained jagged metal, flaming propane and burning timber on the enemy. It also set tree tops ablaze and the fire skipped merrily across the tinder-dry canopy, lighting them like candles on a birthday cake. He ignited two more tanks set up within his gun sights. Up and down the bunker line this was repeated with the same devastating impact. Each explosion triggered a chain reaction and the woods began to quickly glow with massive sheets of fire. Some of the enemy attempted to turn and retreat. The bunker line held fast against this frenzied, desperate rush. They either died on the trail or fled back into the cauldron.

Doug and Joe watched the woods erupt with the rapidly spreading fire. Doug set up the 81mm mortar while Joe managed the ammo. Doug was determined to hit the flanks that Tom was defending in order to slow down the enemy's potential break out.

"You know how to use this?" Joe asked.

"Have some experience from basic training. Of course, that was 1989."

"Can we hit them from here?"

"This baby is good up to 6,000 yards." Doug set the trajectory and launched the first mortar.

Sixty-Four

Rafik struggled to get off the ground. The fire licking at his pant leg provided the needed incentive. He had been stunned and knocked down by a grenade blast that killed the soldier in front him thus sparing his life. Dazed and disoriented he was caught in a man-made hell. The ground was covered by the dead and the cries of the wounded rose like chants from the damned. The fire, fueled by a carpet of dry underbrush, was growing geometrically in scope and intensity. Enemy weapons fire zipped through the area like squadrons of killer bees.

His troops could not hug the ground for cover. They were forced to stand upright and hide behind trees that soon would ignite like torches. He was close enough to see the thin, strung out line of defense in front of him. Attempts to break out in that direction had been slowed by the barricades strung between trees. He had no idea how many of the enemy were behind him. Suddenly his options were further curtailed when mortars began to explode to his right.

Looking left he spotted an avenue of escape. The woods thinned out and ended and it was there that the fire had not yet fully taken its deadly hold. His men rallied around him as he led them to possible safety. As they advanced they saturated the forward ground with weapons fire to disable or set off any remaining traps. When a series of them exploded Rafik's grudging admiration of the Old Infidel returned. The explosions set off more small fires but they had successfully cleared a path out of the woods. Even though they had suffered many casualties there were still more than enough fighters to secure victory because at any moment they would link up with their brothers who were landing on the beach.

Sixty-Five

Will, Bob Canale and Jeff Keifer, the 3rd member of the beach defense team, could hear the distant weapons fire. Their impulse was to join the fight but Wayne had given them a specific mission. Will felt it was a fool's errand to delegate three critically needed fighters to this post based on a hunch. It was a cloudy, moonless night and from their position on the bluffs, all Will could see was black sky meeting black water. A persistent breeze caused the Bay to lap the shore in a steady, up-tempo pace. Then, to Will's ears, there was another sound out there. He asked the others if they heard anything out of synch with the Bay's natural rhythm. They both said no but he wasn't convinced.

"Hand me the flare gun," he said to Bob. "And get ready."

The flare went off with a muffled pop and they watched its red tail travel skyward. When it reached its apogee it exploded, casting a downward drifting red glow that reflected off the Bay's dark water and illuminated the immediate area.

"Motherfucker," Will said in a near yell as the flare revealed several small boats loaded to the gunwales with enemy fighters. They were within 100 feet of shore. Bob slapped Will on the shoulder and pointed to their left. There, coming through the marshland were even more of the enemy.

Will sent up another flare and cocked the BAR. "No mercy. No prisoners," he shouted. The others needed no additional prompting. Weapons fire erupted from all directions. Son-of-a-bitch Will thought to himself. How did he know? Aqaba indeed. He promised himself that if he survived he was going to seriously study military history.

Sixty-Six

The now-raging fire turned a moonless night into a devil's sunrise. Alan saw the enemy gathering in the fish hook and was about to alert Bill to redirect his fire when the horseshoe was struck by rockets launched from the woods' edge. The effort they put into constructing and reinforcing it saved their lives but the top portion was gone and the concussion knocked the three men backwards and covered them in dirt. They quickly scrambled out before it could be fired on again.

"Keep pouring it on. I'll draw their attention." Alan yelled. He grabbed the BAR and began moving towards the fish hook.

Doug and Joe watched their mortar barrage create chaos and death. Despite that and the increasingly lethal fire, the enemy began emerging from the woods. Doug launched the last few mortars which slowed them down temporarily.

"Time to join the party." They grabbed their weapons and left their safe perch.

Despite the fact they had stumbled into a precisely planned ambush, the enemy was poised to break out directly in front of Tom's position. To his left he heard explosions as enemy launched grenades and rockets pinpointed the defenders' different positions. The shrinking of return fire indicated they were devastatingly effective.

It had reached the point where the defenders could no longer hold back a numerically superior force. It seemed they were caught in a scenario right out of the "Sorcerer's Apprentice." For every enemy combatant killed, two seemed to take his place. Tom had the authority to call a retreat. They could move back into the community and fight them house to house. He rejected it. He wouldn't risk giving them free access to the homes sheltering women and children. They would make their stand on this ground.

The forest was being consumed at a rate faster than anyone anticipated. The inferno roared towards them across the treetops and then it made the small leap across the hiking trail and began to devour what remained. Wayne sent word down the line to abandon this position and rush to support the front-line defenders. Josh took a moment to check his watch. What felt like hours of combat had occurred in 20 minutes.

Alan cradled the BAR in his left arm moving and firing on the run. He felt like a latter-day Rambo as he watched the deadly results of his mad solo dash. When enemy fire struck him in his upper leg he couldn't believe how much it hurt. He toppled to the ground but recovered, put the BAR up on its stand and resumed firing on the advancing enemy.

"Come on cocksuckers," he yelled. "Come and get your virgins."

Sixty-Seven

Tom was on the brink. Defensive positions to the left had been wiped out. The MVA administrator was dead. Hassen, Amir and the Dentist were fighting on with no sign of a let up. They had launched every grenade and rocket and had survived equal return fire. They were reduced to using their other weapons sporadically in order to conserve ammunition. Tom actually wondered how people would remember them and honor their memory. Then Wayne and members of the Bunker Brigade poured out from the hiking trail and over the barricades. The enemy scattered through the openings in the defense line into the community.

"Shit, talk about arriving in the nick of time," Tom exclaimed breathlessly.

"You can thank us later," Wayne said. "We've got to get after them."

Doug and Joe arrived at the main battle area in time to watch the enemy overrun several defensive positions. Joe became spastic with fear when he realized the death sounds that surrounded him were coming from friends and neighbors. He wanted to run in any direction that would get him away from the approaching enemy. Yet he stood fast, inspired into fearlessness by the knowledge others had done the same even in the face of their impending deaths. Doug motioned they should separate in a flanking motion to catch the enemy in a crossfire. They staggered themselves so Doug would hit the head of the advance while Joe would attack from the rear.

The enemy had not anticipated encountering resistance once pass the defenders' picket line. As a result, Doug and Joe had an immediate advantage as their attack sowed confusion and disarray. They artfully managed to make two men seem like a platoon. Additional enemy combatants emerging from the woods found themselves attacked by deadly ghosts. In the aftermath of the battle, they would be discovered surrounded by their victims in a kill ratio that redefined courage. In the grand scheme of things, it was a brief firefight but Doug and Joe were two of the rocks upon which Rafik's grand dreams of conquest crashed and vanished.

When they saw Alan go down, Bill and Jim rushed to provide cover and rescue. They were forced to retreat to the horseshoe by a counter attack. The enemy was pressing its numerical superiority when reinforcements arrived. Wayne had divided the Bunker Brigade and sent a detachment under Josh's command to help secure the right flank. It was the enemy's turn to retreat.

"Where are they going?" Josh asked Bill as they watched the enemy run off in the opposite direction.

"I don't know. They didn't even try to swing around behind us. They came out of the woods and went straight in that direction."

"They're heading for the beach."

Joanna and the women sat in darkness listening to sounds of battle. They could see the orange crown of the fire glow in the distance. Quietly wondering what was happening was an unsettling form of torture. Then she spotted them. Several enemy soldiers had gathered at the end of the driveway. More arrived in the courtyard. Theirs was the only occupied home in this courtyard. She watched as they kicked in the doors to several houses, probably looking for hostages. After finding those houses empty, it seemed they were prepared to move on. She could let them and keep everyone safe but she decided against it when her husband's words reminded her that it was their duty, given the opportunity, to kill as many of the enemy as possible.

"Melanie...Katie...get upstairs and be ready. Tell Alison to stay in the safe room with the baby. Don't fire until I start." The girls scrambled upstairs. Cindy moved to Joanna's side.

"Hand me the flashlight."

"What do you have planned?" Cindy asked.

"I'm not quite sure. Let's just see what happens."

Joanna pointed the flashlight towards the window and turned it on. She kept it on for only a few seconds but it served the desired effect.

"They're coming this way. Unlock the front door, get behind it and when I tell you, yank it open."

They approached the home cautiously...several stepped lightly onto the porch....Joanna took Wayne's sawed-off shotgun and lay down in the foyer only a few feet from the front door. She spotted someone peering through the front windows but she avoided detection.

"Get ready," she whispered to Cindy.

They both could hear the footsteps approaching the front door. Cindy saw the doorknob turn.

"They're here."

"Now," Joanna instructed.

Cindy grabbed the door knob and pulled open the front door so wide it crushed her against the wall. Joanna unleashed both barrels and the intruders at the door were launched off the porch and down the steps. Cindy flung the door shut and locked it as return fire slammed the front of house. Joanna went to the window to see the others making a rush for it. Fire from the upstairs slowed them down. Joanna flung open the downstairs windows and made them scatter using the re-loaded shotgun.

"Cover the back."

Cindy moved quickly through the house to the back deck. She spotted a lone gunman turn the corner. She took cover behind the barbeque grill and waited patiently for her target to approach. He walked cautiously at first then sprinted forward, firing as he went. Several rounds hit the barbeque. Cindy emerged from cover and stopped the gunman with two quick bursts.

Will set off flare after flare and under their ghastly illumination his fire team managed to keep the enemy from advancing up the beach. They had come at low tide and the boats became mired in mud a good 20 feet from the shore. The thick muck became their greatest ally. They made ridiculously easy targets. Will and the others were constantly firing on the move to maximize the superiority of their firing positions. In the melee of the battle, Will couldn't distinguish friendly from non-friendly fire but when he felt bullets slam into his back, he became aware of the difference. As he fell, he saw Bob and Jeff go down, too. Even though enemy dead littered the beach, his last thought was wondering if this effort would be viewed as a failure.

Tom and a small detachment were conducting sweeps of the streets and courtyards. He was worried about what havoc the enemy could spread in such close quarters. Everyone's attention was drawn to the sound of weapons fire from the next courtyard. When they arrived on the scene, Tom was stunned to find that combat was occurring in front of Wayne's house. The enemy was quickly suppressed and eliminated.

"Joanna?"

The front door opened and Joanna stepped out. "We're fine. All of us are fine."

"OK," Tom gave the signal to move out.

"Tom, don't tell Wayne. He has a tendency to worry too much."

Even in the midst of the grimmest day in their collective lives, Tom and the others found a reason to laugh.

Sixty-Eight

Fareed listened to the sounds of battle and became increasingly agitated. Using equipment and supplies he had smuggled out of Johns Hopkins Hospital, he converted the downstairs into a mini-operating theatre. Ordered by Wayne and Tom to remain out of the direct conflict, he sat silently in the lantern illuminated space with his wife, Fatima, and Marcy Thorpe, a registered nurse.

He silently seethed against the well-meaning restrictions that were placed on him. His beloved sons, his friends and neighbors were in harm's way and he felt he should be with them. As the sound of gunfire came increasingly closer, Fareed determined his skills as a doctor were meaningless if they were used to save people only so they could live under the merciless boot of extremism.

He quickly removed his scrubs and dressed in dark, camouflage-style clothing. He grabbed his semi-automatic rifle and pistol, doused the lantern, kissed his wife and went looking to kill. He moved silently down the street, remaining in the deep shadows of the houses; becoming motionless when he heard footsteps on the hard pavement. Four men were moving at a brisk in his direction. Fareed gambled and called out to them in Arabic.

"Brothers...I have cornered several American cowards in this house. I need your help."

They responded in Arabic and their words barely left their mouths when Fareed dropped them with an extended burst from his rifle. He paused to allow the sound to stop ringing in his ears when he heard one of the downed men groan. Poking and probing the bodies, he found the one victim who was still alive.

"Why have you killed us? You're one of us."

Fareed spit on the man. "I am not one of you. I am an American!" One shot to the head ended the discussion. Fareed went looking for more. Using the treachery gifted on him by his ability to speak the enemy's language he scored another six kills. He often spoke of it as the greatest night of his life.

Sixty-Nine

Thunder and lightning ripped through the early morning sky as Josh and the other defenders raced through the community towards the beach. Bill had taken the point and yelled to everyone to be ready to engage the enemy immediately. When they entered the playground and picnic area they could see enemy combatants emerging from the beach. They fanned out in a straight line and firing on the run, charged. The enemy stood their ground initially but this time the defenders had equal numbers. Some broke and ran but others laid down their weapons and surrendered. Bill directed some of the fighters to pursue the fleeing enemy while the others rounded up those who had surrendered.

Josh desperately searched for Will among the fallen. He found him face down on the downward slope of the bluff. Josh went to roll him over but hesitated, fearful he might make a critical situation worse.

"Help me, help me," he said to no one in particular.

Bill knelt down with him and helped Josh roll Will over on his back.

"He's still breathing," Bill said.

"Will! Will!" Josh called to him. Will's eyes opened slightly.

"Hey buddy," he answered in a near whisper. "Man, you called it right. It was like a fucking regatta out there."

"Take it easy," Bill advised him. "We'll get you to Fareed's, get you patched up."

"Tell your dad we held them…long enough to make the difference. See…we fucked them up good."

Josh looked out at the beach and the bay. The dead seemed as prevalent as the sand itself.

"Man, I would love being around to celebrate what we did."

"Don't talk anymore," Josh pleaded.

"You know…I turned 45 earlier this year and I got caught up in all that middle-age crisis crap…wondering if my life had meaning. Now, I know it did."

Josh felt life leave Will's body. He was too stunned to cry but fittingly the sky opened and it began raining heavily. The other fighters returned with many of the enemy now captive.

"Bill…what are we going to do with these prisoners?" Jim asked. "We've got no place for them."

"Yes we do. Take them to garbage dump and dispose of them," Bill answered in an angry yet matter-of-fact tone. "Me and Josh will stay here and take care of the wounded."

The prisoners were herded off and disappeared into the playground area.

"Let's get to it," Bill said.

Josh decided to use the revolver he had taken from the Pecora house. He felt it was the appropriate weapon to finally put an end to this business.

Seventy

Wayne and his search party encountered the enemy prisoners being led to the garbage dump. A quick conversation with Jim filled him in on what had happened. Throughout the area, the sound of weapons fire had been replaced by the thunder and lightning of a powerful, late summer storm. Wayne gave everyone the option of continuing to search for enemy stragglers or to go check on their families and resume the search. They all chose the latter leaving Wayne alone to conduct the search. He heard from several people that the remaining enemy combatants had scattered and ran off so he wasn't too concerned as he continued to work the neighborhood's dark corners.

He heard the click of the chamber being cocked and loaded. It came from the narrow gap between two newer homes. He instinctively turned his body sideways to make himself less of a target. The bullet slammed his right shoulder and knocked him to the ground. Wayne's first reaction was anger. He had fought for nearly two years in Vietnam with only a few nicks and scratches. Now, it seemed he might die three blocks from home. Even though it was approaching sunrise, the thunderstorm kept the skies a smoky gray. Wayne squinted at the gunman moved out into the open.

"Well, I wondered where you had gotten to," Wayne said as a greeting.

"Get up," Rafik ordered.

"Help me, I'm wounded."

"You know it's just a flesh wound."

"Why so generous?" Wayne asked as he lifted himself off the ground.

"I couldn't let you die before realizing that in some small way, I was your conqueror."

"Still the glory-seeking little boy, aren't you? Well, live or die, at least I proved that as a commanding officer, you're a total zero. An attack from the water? Really? How many men did you lose? 50? 60? Killed by just three! Stupid…stupid…stupid. I can't even take credit for it. You were outmaneuvered by a 17-year-old. You had us beat. We were outnumbered, outgunned. The only way we could win is if you fucked up. And boy did you ever! I can explain all the ways you fucked up. Do you want me to go alphabetically or chronologically?

Rafik raised his revolver and pointed it directly at Wayne.

"Any last words?"

"Fuck you…and everyone like you."

Three shots rang out. Wayne reacted in anticipation of being struck. Instead, he watched Rafik lurch forward then fall face first into a growing puddle of water. In the misty early morning gloom, Wayne spotted another gunman. He scrambled to retrieve his weapon as this anonymous gunman moved forward, his weapon at the ready.

"Are you OK, Mr. Foltz?"

"Randy? What in the world? How did you happen to be back there?"

"I was hiding. I was down near the woods fighting but Mr. Larimore and Mr. Higgins got shot…I think they're dead. I was scared so I ran. I went inside the house to get out of the rain. I looked out back and saw him," he pointed to Rafik. "He was moving through the backyard and when I saw you out front, I figured he was following you."

He paused and took a deep breath.

"So, when he went around the side, I came out to see what he was up to. And then, he shot you….and he was going to kill you, I had to do something." He paused, wondering if killing Rafik would redeem him for his earlier cowardice. He began crying and spoke through muffled sobs.

"You won't tell people that I ran and hid, will you?"

Wayne gave him a reassuring hug. "No…no one ever needs to know."

"I just didn't have the courage. Even after everything they did to my family."

"Randy, people find their courage eventually. Fortunately for me, you found yours at the right time."

"Yea, it is weird that I'd be the one to save you."

"C'mon, I'll make sure you get home safely."

They walked without speaking and as they got close to his house, Randy handed his weapon to Wayne.

"I don't ever want to shoot another person again."

"Neither do I, son. I'm too old for this much excitement."

EPILOGUE

Sixteen months later: Wayne finished wrapping the last Christmas present and put it under the tree. He had trouble finding a spot for it but the fact there was a tree and presents were enough to make him believe once again in goodwill towards men.

There were many things this Christmas for which he was grateful. His son, Charlie, had returned from the Arabian campaign, full of stories on how Iran had been reduced to dust. He and Alison, who was expecting their second child, moved into one of the unoccupied and unclaimed homes in the community. Soon after Charley's return, Cindy was set up on a blind date with a member of her brother's wing group. Now, they were engaged and had also moved into another unoccupied and unclaimed house. Most of the residents who fled never returned.

Wayne checked under the tree for presents with his name. Compared to what was designated for Emily, the other kids and young adults, he definitely wasn't getting his fair share. Yet, he already received the finest Christmas present of his life when Josh, Melanie and Katie had their last name legally changed to Foltz. It was Josh's idea but they all embraced it enthusiastically.

The highlight of Christmas Day would be the formal dedication of the cemetery where the community's 43 fallen defenders now were buried. The fire had consumed the majority of the woods but nature had reclaimed and transformed the area into a lush meadow. The cemetery with its polished and gleaming headstones was situated in the area once known as the fishhook. Tom, now Governor of Maryland, would preside over the ceremony and deliver the keynote address. Then he and his wife, daughter, son-in-law and grandson would join the Foltz household for Christmas dinner.

Tom's gubernatorial campaign was nearly derailed by accusations from an anonymous source that he participated in executing defenseless enemy combatants who had either surrendered or were wounded. A combined civilian and military commission formed to investigate these charges found several mass graves containing the remains of enemy combatants on the grounds of Chesapeake Heights. The bodies had been incinerated and in sworn testimony renowned Hopkins surgeon, Dr. Fareed Akbari informed the commission that he personally ordered the mass cremation because of health-related concerns and to prevent the spread of disease. The commission concluded, given the state of the corpses, there was no way to conclusively determine if they actually were executed or died as a result of combat. Additionally, they ruled that as civilians, the defenders were not bound by the Geneva Convention or other articles of warfare. They also noted in their final report that they could not find any eyewitnesses to corroborate the charges. Ironically, instead of damaging his campaign, the investigation elevated Tom to hero status and he won in a landslide.

And theirs was not an isolated story, either. Across the country, makeshift civilian armies and militias had sprung up and checkmated the enemy with a combination of heroism and savagery. Yet, despite some caterwauling from isolated sources, these actions were met with praise and applause. The American people had lost their appetite for self blame and recrimination.

If any good came out of this disaster, Wayne would recount later, the feckless ideologies that had contributed so much to the country's near downfall were totally discredited. Telling the truth was back in fashion.

Even though it was Christmas, peace on earth remained a tenuous proposition. In a nationally televised Christmas address, President David Petraeus expressed optimism that marital law would be lifted by spring. Domestic terrorists and their enablers had killed millions of Americans. Civil unrest, looting and lawlessness not directly linked to terrorism, added to the toll of death and destruction. Detroit existed only as a name and a pile of rubble. Sections of New York City, Los Angeles, Chicago, Washington, DC, Baltimore and Minneapolis were uninhabitable. Nearly every major American city had suffered some level of catastrophic destruction.

President Petraeus also announced that some American troops would be withdrawn from Mexico now that his administration was confident they had stamped out the narco-terrorist/Islamic forces that had waged war all through the Southwest. He added that the on-going annexation of Mexican territory along the US border would continue as well as the creation of a 100 mile "no-go" buffer zone. The razing of every Mexican city and town within that zone, including Tijuana and Ciudad Juarez, and the displacement of its populations would continue. Popular sentiment even favored extending the invasion to Venezuela when it was learned that Hugo Chavez had allowed the IRG to use his country as a staging ground plus supplied the terrorists with men and materials. That, the President assured everyone, would be dealt with in the near future.

The most controversial part of the presidential Christmas address was the announcement of a full pardon for former President Obama. He claimed the mistakes made by the former president were ones of well-intended but misguided policies and didn't rise to the level of impeachable offenses. President Petraeus added the goal of his administration was to re-build a new America and the trial of a former president would hinder that task by re-igniting old divisions and passions. Several weeks later the White House announced the former First Family had accepted an invitation from the Spanish Royal Family to temporarily relocate in Spain as their guests.

Several years later Obama died in a one-car accident. His chauffeured vehicle mysteriously ran off the road on a bright sunny day, struck a tree and burst into flames. A joint inquest by the American and Spanish governments concluded it was, finally, an unfortunate accident with no foul play involved. The suspicion always lingered that the "unfortunate accident" was the handiwork of the Mossad under the direct instructions of the Israeli government. Time could not heal the grief and anger of the tiny nation that lost 2.2 million of its citizens.

The political situation in other parts of the world was decidedly worse. Muslims in Europe became fatally acquainted with the continent's historic affinity for genocide. South Korea's defeat of the north triggered a huge south-bound exodus with uncounted numbers ending up in the miserable conditions of internment camps. But in Chesapeake Heights, things were on an upswing. Wayne referred to himself as "semi-retired". He occasionally did custom woodwork and carpentry but he now spent the majority of his time with Emily and his children. He and Joanna were closer than ever. She also was busier than ever, counseling scores of locals who were suffering from different levels of post traumatic stress syndrome.

Josh never went back to skateboarding or video game playing. He continued his passion for history and had serious discussions with Charlie about the possibility of attending the recently reopened United States Naval Academy.

The house was quiet. All was in order. Wayne went downstairs where he had converted part of the family room into an artist's studio. Infused with the spirit of the holiday, he decided to play Christmas music and found an appropriate channel on the satellite radio player. He approached a large canvas sitting on an easel and studied it. He was content that the images of Doug, Alan, Will, Joe and Bob were honest and true, even though in some cases, they were drawn from memory. They were the focal point of this painting that would be a visual tribute to the 43 friends and neighbors who sacrificed all to halt the rampage of raw tyranny.

He shuffled through the photos given to him by family members. In just about every instance, the face looking back at him was smiling, beaming with life and joy. Their acts of courage were as profound as any he had experienced and he was determined that they would not be forgotten.

This painting was designated as the centerpiece of his first gallery show and sale. He already received several substantial offers based solely on the description in the show catalogue. He wouldn't sell it for any amount and actually didn't care if anything sold. It only mattered that after decades of waiting, he finally was given the opportunity to publically display his paintings.

As he worked on the canvas, the holiday music jumped to the foreground of Wayne's consciousness with the playing of the "Hallelujah" chorus from Handel's "Messiah." As the words "And He shall reign forever and forever" rang out, Wayne recalled the conversation with Rafik on the eve of battle. He mocked Rafik's religion, predicting it was doomed to inevitable failure, for purely strategic reasons. In the aftermath of their victory and eventual rescue by elements of the 82nd Airborne, Wayne had ample opportunity to sort out what inspired that impromptu prediction. Eventually, he concluded that a religious ideology dedicated to oppressing the human inspiration inherent in the creation of art, literature, music… to the concept of joy itself; that focused chiefly on death and destruction would inevitably sag under the weight of so much wasted human potential. It was conversations with Fareed, a man who joyfully embraced America that brought the answers into sharp and clear focus.

"Freedom," he told Wayne, "allows us to pursue noble ambitions and higher glories. Freedom, to borrow a phrase from Lincoln, allows us to be better angels."

What he spoke that day to Rafik came from a deep, untapped reservoir of belief that the history of Western Civilization was, despite all flaws, one of personal liberation that merited defense to the death. Those that stood together through the crisis were those who knew this intuitively.

"Remember, my friend," Fareed said, "you were a leader in two wars because you believe in freedom."

His first war made him a pariah. His second war made him a hero. Wayne's life had come full circle. He could not have wished for a better outcome.

THE END

About the Author

The novel "American Jihad Rising" combines Michael Elliott's love of writing with his intense interest in politics and current events. An award-winning advertising copywriter and commercial broadcast producer, Mr. Elliott spent several years writing movie screenplays via The William Morris Agency. His interest in Islamic-inspired terrorism began when he witnessed the destruction of the World Trade Center Twin Towers from just across the Hudson River in New Jersey. The spark that produced this novel started in 2009 when he became acquainted with military members of the Defense Department's Counter Terrorism Unit headquartered in the Pentagon. The things he learned convinced him the dangers posed by international and domestic terrorism were even greater than he had originally imagined. As he developed the novel's various scenarios, he reviewed them with a military expert who had in-depth knowledge of terrorist networks and their plans. He was told his scenarios not only were plausible but likely to unfold in the near future.

Mr. Elliott lives in his hometown of Annapolis, MD. He holds a BA in English from McDaniel College and a MA in Journalism from Penn State University.